Careless

···

Bianca Solomon

Contents

ONE

- -

Tara rested her head against Will's shoulder as Joyce drove them to the arcade.

After all the events that had occurred last year, Joyce took Twelve in as her own.

The car slowly halted to a stop as Tara lifted her head from her brother's shoulder.

"Okay so, I'll pick you both up in two hours. That's 9:00 on the dot, okay?" Joyce told them as Will helped Tara with her seat belt.

"Yes."

"Okay."

"If anything happens, if you need to come home, just ask them to use their phone and call home. Okay?" Joyce told them. "Don't-"

"Don't walk or bike home. I know." Will cut her off while opening the car door.

"Okay but guys-" Joyce started with a concerned expression.

"Mom, we have to go!" Will exclaimed impatiently.

"Have fun." She responded with a smile.

Will stepped out of the car as did Tara.

They jogged up to their friends.

"To slay the dragon, use the magic sword," The game character instructed.

"Oh Jesus, I'm in uncharted territory here guys!" Dustin exclaimed dramatically.

"Down!" They all yelled.

"I'm going, I'm going!" Dustin yelled back while pulling down a lever.

It wasn't long before his character turned into ashes and fell dead.

"No, no no! I hate this overpriced bullshit!" Dustin exclaimed full of frustration. "Son of a bitch! Piece of shit!"

If she was being honest, Tara could care less about the Arcade. She only wanted to hang out with her friends.

"You're not nimble enough," Lucas told Dustin with a smirk. "But you'll get there one day. But until then, Princess Daphne is still mine!"

"Whatever. I'm still tops on Centipede and Dig Dug." Dustin responded.

"You sure about that?" A voice said from behind them.

They all turned around to find Keith.

"Sure about what?" Dustin asked.

Dustin's smile dropped.

"You're kidding me." He murmured as he raced over to Dig Dug's game machine.

They all rushed after him.

"No!" Dustin yelled out of frustration as his eyes ran down the scoreboard.

Somebody named MadMax had a higher score than him.

Tara squinted her eyes, trying to read the numbers.

"751,300 points!" Will exclaimed, his eyes enlarging.

"That's impossible." Mike said.

"Who is Mad Max?" Dustin asked Keith.

"Better than you." Keith replied, watching in amusement as Dustin flipped him his middle finger.

"Is it you?" Will asked.

"You know I despise Dig Dug." Keith responded with a scoff.

"Then who is it?" Lucas pressed.

"Yeah, spill it Keith!" Dustin added impatiently.

"You want information, then I need something in return." Keith responded as he turned to Mike.

"No, no way! You're not getting a date with her!" Mike exclaimed.

"Mike, come on. Just get him the date." Lucas said.

"I'm not prostituting my sister!" Mike replied.

"But it's for a good cause." Lucas continued.

"No, don't get him the date," Dustin spoke. "Know what? He's gonna spread his nasty ass rash to your whole family."

"Acne isn't a rash and it isn't contagious, you prepubescent waistoid." Keith insulted him.

"Oh, I'm a waistoid?" Dustin asked, his eyes enlarging. "She wouldn't go on a date with you. You make what? $2.50 an hour?"

"Nice perm." Keith snapped back.

Tara listened intently as Dustin continued to insult Keith.

It was the next day, and also Tara's first day of school at Hawkins Middle.

Joyce wanted to wait until Tara's hair was at a good length that nobody would question.

"Meet the human brain," Mr. Clarke said to his class full of students. "I know it doesn't look like much. A little gross even? But consider this! There are a hundred billion cells inside of this miracle of evolution."

"No I did not misspeak. I did not stutter. A hundred billon!" He excitedly explained.

The door suddenly opened as the Principal walked in. Behind him was a redheaded girl.

"Ah, this must be our other new student." Mr. Clarke said with a smile.

"Indeed it is. All yours." The Principal spoke before exiting the room.

The girl attempted to find a seat but Mr. Clarke stopped her.

"All right, hold up. You don't get away that easy." He told her.

She rolled her eyes before stopping.

"Dustin, drum roll." Mr. Clarke instructed.

Tara watched as Dustin brought out a heavy leather book and placed it onto his desk.

He began hitting his fists against the book as if making a drum-roll sound.

"Class, please welcome all the way from sunny California, the latest passenger to join us on our curiosity voyage, Maxine!" Mr. Clarke introduced.

"It's Max." She quickly said.

"I'm sorry?" Mr. Clarke asked in confusion.

"Nobody calls me Maxine. It's Max." She said.

Dustin's smile dropped.

"Mad Max." Dustin and Lucas whispered together in unison.

"Well, all aboard Max!" Mr. Clarke said with a smile.

The five Party members watched as Max found a seat and sat down.

After school, they watched through a gate as Max practiced on her skateboard.

"There's no way that's Mad Max." Mike spoke.

"Yeah. Girls don't play video games." Will said.

"And even if they did, you can't get 750,300 points on Dig Dug." Mike said. "It's impossible."

"But her name is Max." Lucas said.

"So?" Mike responded.

"So... How many Maxes do you know?" Lucas asked him.

"I don't know." Mike replied.

"Zero! That's how many." Lucas responded for him.

"And she shows up at school the day after someone with her same name breaks our top score." Dustin said. "I mean, you kidding me?"

"Exactly. So she's gotta be Mad Max. She's gotta be." Lucas agreed.

"And plus, she skateboards, so she's pretty awesome." Dustin added.

"Awesome." Tara repeated.

"Awesome? You guys haven't even spoken a word to her." Mike told them.

"I don't have to- Shit! I've lost the target." Dustin cursed.

They scanned the area for the redheaded girl.

"Oh! There." Will said as he pointed.

Max was walking up the steps.

She dropped a piece of paper into the trash can.

They all rushed towards the trash can.

Dustin dug through the trash before picking up her piece of paper.

"Got it." Dustin said before opening up the crumpled piece of paper.

"Stop spying on me, creeps." They all read together.

"Well shit." Dustin cursed.

"Bad?" Tara asked innocently.

TWO

They all rode their bikes to school, in their Ghostbusters costumes.

Tara dressed as a Ghost. She placed a bed sheet over her body with cut out holes for her eyes.

"Woah woah." Mike said as he turned to Lucas. "Why are you Venkman?"

"Because I'm Venkman." Lucas replied.

"No, I'm Venkman!" Mike argued.

"Why can't there just be two Venkmans?" Will asked to which Tara nodded to.

"Because there's only one Venkman in real life. We planned this months ago; I'm Venkman, Dustin's Stanz, you're Egon, and you're Winston!" Mike explained.

"I specifically didn't agree to Winston." Lucas told him.

"Yes you did!" Mike argued.

"I don't think he did." Will said.

"No one wants to be Winston." Lucas said.

"Why not?" Tara asked.

"Why not? He joined the team super late, he's not funny and he's not even a scientist!" Lucas explained.

"Yeah but he's still cool." Mike said.

"If he's so cool then you be Winston." Lucas responded back.

"I can't!" Mike quickly said.

"Why not?" Lucas asked him.

"B-Because," Mike stuttered.

"Because you're not black?" Lucas said for him.

"I didn't say that." Mike defended.

"But you thought it!" Lucas said.

While they argued, Dustin began trailing away from them and stopped in his tracks.

"Guys!" He yelled, breaking their fight.

"Why is no one else wearing costumes?" He asked.

The bell rang for school.

As they walked through the hallway, a couple kids laughed at them.

"When do people make these decisions?" Dustin asked.

"Everyone dressed up last year." Will recalled.

"It's a conspiracy, I'm telling you." Dustin said.

"Just be cool." Mike told them.

"Who you gonna call? The nerds!" One kid teased.

After school, they approached Max at her locker.

Dustin cleared his throat to get her attention.

"Hi, Max. I'm Dustin and this is-" Dustin greeted her.

"Lucas and Tara." Lucas said while gesturing to himself and Tara.

"Yeah I know," Max paused. "The stalkers."

"Stalkers?" Tara asked with a small head tilt.

"N-No, actually we weren't stalking you." Lucas denied.

"No, we were just concerned because you're new and all." Dustin lied.

"Yeah, for your safety." Lucas added.

"There are a lot of bullies here." Dustin said.

"So many bullies, it's crazy." Lucas said.

"Is that why you're wearing proton packs?" Max asked, eyeing their costumes.

"Well, these don't function, but," Dustin paused as he brought out his trap. "I do have this handy dandy little trap here. And look, it even opens and closes. Look!"

He made the trap open and close.

Max remained unimpressed.

"It's cool right? No? Okay. So, we were talking last night and you're new here so you probably don't have any friends to take you trick or treating and you're scared of bullies, so we were thinking that it'd be okay if you come with us." Dustin told her.

"It'd be okay?" Max asked.

"Yeah! Our party's a democracy and the majority voted you could come." Dustin said.

"I didn't realize it was such an honor to go trick or treating with you!" Max said sarcastically.

"We know where to get the full sized candy bars." Dustin replied. "We figured you'd want in."

"That's presumptuous of you." Max said.

Tara just smiled.

"Yeah, totally! Uh, so you'll come?" Dustin asked her.

"Please." Tara added.

Max rolled her eyes before walking away.

"We're meeting at the Maple street cul-de-sac at 7:00!" Dustin yelled to her.

"Presumptuous." Dustin repeated proudly. "That's a good thing, right?"

Lucas inhaled deeply before walking down the hallway.

"Listen. Stay close to your brother, okay?" Joyce told Tara and Will who were ready to walk out the door.

Tara nodded with an eager smile.

"And listen, if you've got a bad feeling or anything, you tell him to take you straight home. You promise?" Joyce asked.

Will put his thumb up.

"You ready, guys?" Jonathan asked them.

They walked out the door.

"Be safe." Joyce said.

"I hope it doesn't suck!" Bob said, imitating Dracula. She had gotten pretty close to Bob. He was like a father figure to her, in a way.

"I just don't get what she sees in him," Jonathan rambled. "Bob."

"I like him." Tara said.

"At least he doesn't treat me different," Will said. "I mean, Tara and I can't even go trick or treating by ourselves, it's lame."

"You think I'm lame?" Jonathan asked him.

"No, but it's not like Nancy's coming to watch over Mike." Will explained.

Once Jonathan had parked at Mike's, he took a deep breath.

"If I let you guys go on your own, you promise to stay in the neighborhood?" Jonathan asked them.

"Yes." Tara agreed.

"And be back at Mike's by 9:00." Jonathan added.

"9:30?" Will asked hopefully.

"9:00." Jonathan repeated himself.

Will opened the car door for Tara and him, and they got out.

To say Tara was excited was an understatement. She'd never been trick or treating before, because she was locked up in a Lab for most of her life.

"'Trick or treat!" They all said as they knocked on the first door.

"Awh!" A lady awed. "Well, aren't you cute? The little exterminators and their pet!"

They all shook it off and grabbed a handful of candy.

"If I get another three muskateers, I'm gonna kill myself." Lucas joked.

"What's wrong with three muskateers?" Dustin asked.

"No one likes three muskateers." Mike said.

"Yeah, it's just Nougat." Will said.

"Woah, just nougat? It is top three for me!" Dustin defended.

"Top three?" Lucas asked in disbelief.

"Top three!" Dustin repeated himself.

"Oh god, give me a break." Mike complained.

"Seriously, I can just eat a bowl of Nougat, straight up." Dustin said.

A figure suddenly came out of nowhere with a knife, it lunged at them.

They all jumped back.

Tara let out a frightened yelp as she hid behind Will.

Lucas on the other hand, let out a high pitched scream.

The figure took off their hood, revealing Max.

"Holy shit! You should've seen the look on your faces!" She giggled before turning to Lucas.

"And you? Who screams like that? You sound like a little girl." She teased before beginning to walk off, leaving the five of them speechless.

"Hey, you guys coming or not? Ooh! I heard we should hit up Loch Nora; that's where the rich people live right?" Max added.

They all followed after her.

"Another full size. Like seriously, rich people are such suckers!" Dustin exclaimed in delight. "Wait, you're not rich, right?"

"No, I live up old cherry road." Max replied.

"Oh." Dustin said.

"No, it's fine. I mean, the street's good for skating." Max said.

"Yeah, totally tubular." Dustin said.

Lucas, Max and Tara looked at him blankly.

"What? Did I say that right?" Dustin asked.

"It's like, totally tubular!" Lucas said, his tone sounding like a surfers. "What a gnarly wave, dude."

"Stop, my ears are hurting!" Max exclaimed with a smile.

"Hey, guys?" Max called out.

They stopped in their tracks.

"Your friend," She pointed to Mike who was rushing off.

They all glanced at one another before deciding to follow him.

Mike ran up to Will, who was hugging his knees, his eyes enlarged with fright.

"Is he okay?" Lucas asked Mike.

"I don't know," Mike responded as he helped Will up to his feet. "I'm gonna get you home."

Tara followed before looking at her friends once more.

"Bye." She said.

She wanted to continue trick or treating, but she was worried for whatever happened with Will.

"It's like I'm stuck." Will explained.

"Like stuck in the Upside Down?" Mike asked.

"No. You know on a view master when it gets..." Will paused to think of the right word.

"Caught between two slides?" Mike asked.

"Yeah, like that. Like one side's our world and the other slide is the upside down." Will explained. "And there was this noise coming from everywhere. And then I saw something."

"Demogorgon?" Mike and Tara asked in unison.

"No." Will said. "It was like this huge shadow in the sky. Only, it was alive. And it was coming for me."

Tara fiddled with her hoodie sleeves, feeling a sudden wave of guilt that she couldn't help him.

"Is this all real? Or is it like the doctors say, all in your head?" Mike asked him.

"I don't know," Will replied. "Just please don't tell the others. They won't understand."

"I do." Tara said.

"And so would Eleven." Mike said.

"She would?" Will asked.

"She always did." Mike said.

THREE

"Was that you guys I heard milling around last night or was that a ghost?" Bob asked as he drove.

"Me, probably." Will responded.

"Was sleeping." Tara said.

"Another nightmare?" Bob asked.

"No." Will lied.

"Did I ever tell you guys about Mr. Baldo?" Bob asked the dynamic duo.

Tara tilted her head in interest.

"I was a little younger than you guys," Bob explained. "Standing in line for the Ferris wheel at the roane county fair. And suddenly, I feel this fat white glove tap me on the shoulder. I spin around and there he is. Mr. Baldo."

"Hey, kiddo! Would you like a balloon?" Bob said, sounding like a clown. "Go ahead! Laugh; it's funny!"

A small smile crept upon Tara's lips.

"It wasn't funny back then, I can tell you that." Bob added. "I couldn't get him out of my head. Every night, he would come to me in my dreams. And every night when he came to me, I ran. It got so bad that I made my mom stay in the room with me until I could fall asleep every night."

"Really?" Will asked.

"Really." Bob said. "It went on like that for months. And then one day, the nightmares suddenly stopped. Wanna know how?"

"How?" Will and Tara asked in unison.

Tara had nightmares, quite frequently, about the Lab. Papa. And his cruel punishments/tests. She found comfort in the fact she'd never see him again, though.

"Well, I fell asleep. And just like always, Mr. Baldo came to me. Only this time I didn't run. This time, I stood my ground. I just looked at Mr. Baldo in his stupid face and I said, go away. And just like that, he was gone." Bob finished explaining. "Never saw him again. Easy peasy, right?"

"Easy peasy." Will said.

"Just like that." Bob said as he snapped his fingers.

Bob parked the car outside the school.

"Have a great day, kids." He said as they hopped out the car.

"Thanks." Tara said.

"The case of Phineas Gage is one of the great medical curiosities of all time." Mr. Clarke said to his class full of students. "Phineas was a railroad worker in 1848 who had a nightmarish accident. A large iron road was driven completely through his head. Phineas miraculously survived. He seemed fine; and physically yes, he was. But his injury resulted in a complete change to his personality."

Tara felt eyes at the back of her head and turned around, only to find Max staring at her.

Max quickly diverted her gaze to the school windows.

"...At the time this was known as the american crowbar case. Although it wasn't a-" Mr. Clarke got cut off when the classroom door loudly opened.

Dustin rushed inside and to his seat.

"I am so sorry, Mr. Clarke." Dustin said between panting. "Please continue with the class."

"Although it wasn't a crowbar, it was a rod, as I said." Mr. Clarke continued.

"We have to meet, all of us. AV Club, lunch." Dustin whispered to his friends.

"Yes." Tara said.

"Why?" Mike asked.

"I have something that you won't believe." Dustin replied quietly.

Then he turned to Max.

"Av club. Lunch." He whispered in her direction.

Max leaned as close as she could to hear him better.

"Dustin." Mr. Clarke called.

"Yes, my lord?" Dustin turned back around to face Mr. Clarke.

"Please yes." Dustin immediately said.

"The case of Phineas Gage." Mr. Clarke reminded him.

"Phineas Gage." Dustin repeated while bringing out one of his school books.

"Page 104." Mr. Clarke said.

"104... 104..." Dustin repeated as he searched through the book.

"Focus." Mr. Clarke instructed.

"Focusing." Dustin said in response.

"AV club." Dustin whispered to Max once more.

She put a sarcastic thumbs up.

He just smiled at her.

At AV, Dustin opened up his trap.

To their surprise, inside was some sort of slug.

"His name is D'Artagnan." Dustin introduced before picking up the creature in his hands. "Cute right?"

"D'Artagnan?" Mike asked with confusion.

"Dart for short." Dustin said.

"And he was in your trash?" Max asked.

"Foraging for food." Dustin replied. "You wanna hold him?"

Max's eyes widened.

"No-" She quickly began to protest.

"He doesn't bite." Dustin told her.

"I don't want to-" She got cut off when Dart crawled onto her hand.

She grimaced in disgust and handed him to Tara.

Tara froze in disgust and Dart slithered onto Lucas's hand.

"Ugh, he's like a living booger." Lucas insulted while passing Dart onto Will's palm.

"Oh god!" Will exclaimed as he gave Dart to Mike.

Mike wasn't even fazed. He leaned closer at Dart, examining it.

"What is he?" He asked.

"My question exactly." Dustin responded, which wasn't an exact answer.

Dustin placed a couple books onto the table.

"At first, I thought it was some type of Pollywog." Dustin started.

"Pollywog?" Max and Tara asked in unison.

"It's another word for a tadpole. A tadpole is the larval stage of a toad-" Dustin explained, narrowing it down for them.

"I know what a tadpole is." Max quickly cut him off.

"All right, then you know that most tadpoles are aquatic, right?" Dustin asked.

Tara shook her head.

"Well Dart isn't. He doesn't need water." Dustin said.

"Yeah but aren't there non aquatic pollywogs?" Lucas asked.

"Terrestrial pollywogs? Yep, two to be exact. Indirana semipalmata and the Adenomera andreae. One's from India, one's from south america. So how did one end up in my trash?" Dustin ponders aloud.

"Maybe some scientists brought it here and it escaped?" Max suggested.

"Do you guys see that?" Mike asked as he leaned closer to Dart's level. "Looks like something is moving inside of it."

They all peered closer at the slug.

Mike grabbed the light and directed it at Dart.

Dart screeched loudly, making all of them jump back.

"There's another thing," Dustin said. "Reptiles, they're cold blooded. Ectothermic right? They love heat, the sun... Dart hates it. It hurts him."

"So if he's not a pollywog or a reptile..." Lucas began.

"Then I've discovered a new species." Dustin finished his sentence, making everyone's eyes widen.

The bell rung, and everyone dashed out of the AV room like a bat out of hell.

"We gotta show him to Mr. Clarke." Lucas said.

"No, what if he steals my discovery?" Dustin asked, his tone laced with panic.

"Won't let him." Tara assured him.

"You know, I'm thinking of calling it, Dustonious Pollywogus." Dustin said proudly before turning to the two girls. "What do you think?"

Tara simply nodded.

"I think you're an idiot." Max commented as a response to Dustin.

"Y'know, when I become rich and famous for this one day, don't come crawling back to me saying, Oh my god Dustin, I am so sorry for being mean to you back in eighth grade." Dustin said in a girly voice.

"This is the reason I was late for class," Dustin revealed, placing his trap onto Mr. Clarke's desk.

"Pretty neat. These doors function?" Mr. Clarke asked.

"Well yeah obviously, but it's not about the trap. It's about what's inside." Dustin responded. "Now this very well may change your perception of the world."

"Consider my interest piqued." Mr. Clarke said.

"All right, first, let's just clarify that this is my discovery, not yours." Dustin told him.

"Dustin, jesus, just show him!" Lucas exclaimed out of frustration.

"I'm just trying to clarify-" Dustin tried.

"Dustin!" Max exclaimed.

"Please." Tara added.

"Okay fine." Dustin reluctantly said as he reached for his trap.

At that moment, the door swung open.

"Stop!" Mike yelled at the top of his lungs as he rushed inside the class-room. "I'm really sorry, Mr. Clarke, it was just a stupid prank."

Mike grabbed the trap in a rush.

"What the hell are you doing?" Dustin asked with annoyance.

"Mike?" Tara asked.

"I told him to stop; we need to go. Right now." Mike instructed as he began taking steps out of the classroom along with Will.

"Right now!" Mike yelled, more of a demand this time.

They all ran out of the classroom, leaving a very confused Mr. Clarke.

Max repeatedly hit her fist against the door, trying to open it.

But to no avail.

The door was locked.

They were huddled in one corner, in the AV room.

"I don't understand," Lucas started off.

"What do you not understand?" Mike asked him.

"Will saw something that looked like Dart last year?" Lucas asked.

"Kind of but there was no tail." Will replied.

"But then he heard it yesterday. The exact same sound." Mike said.

"Why didn't you tell us before?" Dustin asked Will, a little annoyed.

"I wasn't sure." Will replied.

"So, it's a coincidence." Dustin quickly said.

"Or not," Mike said. "What if when Will was stuck in the upside down, he somehow acquired true sight?"

"True sight?" Lucas and Tara asked in unison.

"It gives you the power to see into the ethereal plane." Dustin explained.

"Elaborate." Lucas asked with a sigh.

"Maybe these episodes that Will keeps having aren't really flashbacks at all. Maybe they're real. Maybe Will can somehow see into the upside down." Mike spoke.

"Bad." Tara whispered in realization.

Mike nodded.

"So that would mean..." Lucas began.

"Dart is from the upside down." Mike finished his sentence for him.

"We have to take him to Hopper." Lucas said with a sigh.

"I agree." Mike said.

"No way!" Dustin immediately said. "If we take him to Hopper, Dart's as good as dead."

"Maybe he should be." Mike said.

"How can you say that?" Dustin asked in disbelief.

"How can you not? He's from the upside down!" Mike exclaimed.

"Maybe. But even if he is, that doesn't automatically mean that he's bad." Dustin said.

"That's like saying just because someone's from the death star doesn't make them bad." Mike snapped.

"We have a bond." Dustin said.

"A bond? Just because he likes nougat?" Mike said.

"No because he trusts me!" Dustin snapped at Mike.

"He trusts you?" Lucas asked with uncertainty.

"Yes, I promised that I would take care of him." Dustin explained.

Dart suddenly screeched; wriggling around in the trap.

Max continued to bang her fist at the door.

She reached over at her backpack and pulled out a hair pin.

She carefully placed the pin inside of the door lock, to pick-lock the door.

Mike grabbed an object, and aimed it at Dart, defensively.

"Don't hurt him!" Dustin warned him.

"Only if he attacks!" Mike replied.

"Just open it already!" Lucas demanded Dustin.

"I can." Tara said while tilting her head to the side.

The trap opened, thanks to Tara's powers.

Dart rolled out of the trap and onto the table.

"Holy shit!" Lucas cursed under his breath.

Two legs popped out of Dart's body, slime getting everywhere.

Mike rammed at Dart.

"No!" Dustin yelled with panic.

Tara held Mike in place with her powers, for Dustin. She could tell Dustin had something with Dart.

"Tara-" Mike groaned in annoyance.

"I'm sorry." Tara whispered as Dustin mouthed a quick thank you her way.

Dart slithered out onto the floor as Tara released her hold on Mike.

Tara felt drained but shook it off. Now wasn't the time.

Max managed to unlock the door, and much to her surprise, Dart ran out of the classroom and out into the school halls.

Dustin raced out of the room and knocked Max down.

She squirmed under his body before they both stood up.

"What was that?" She asked.

"Dart!" Mike said while raising his voice.

"What?" She asked.

"You let him escape!" Mike blamed Max.

"Why did you try to attack him?" Dustin asked Mike.

"Come on," Mike said with a sigh as they all ran down the school halls, on search for a slug.

Tara wandered into the school gymnasium with Max.

"Here." Max said as she went into the boys' bathroom. "Oh, not here-"

A noise behind them caused them to jump fresh out of their skins.

Mike lunged at them with an oar.

Once he realized it was them, he dropped the oar.

"What the hell are you doing?" Max asked.

"What are you doing?" Mike asked Max. "Why are you in here?"

"Looking for Dart." Max replied.

"This is the boys' room." Mike pointed out.

"So?" Max responded.

"So you should go home!" Mike said out of annoyance as he walked off.

Tara and Max followed.

"Why do you hate me so much?" Max asked Mike finally.

"I don't hate you. How can I hate you? I don't even know you." Mike responded.

"Yeah but you don't want me in your party." Max said.

"Correct." Mike said.

"Why not?" Max asked.

"Because you're annoying." Mike snapped at her. "Also we don't need another Party member! I'm our Paladin, Will's our Cleric, Dustin's our Bard, Lucas is our ranger and El and Tara are our mages."

Tara's heart stopped at the mention of her sister's name. She missed El. A lot.

"El? Who's El?" Max questioned.

"Someone. No one." Mike quickly replied.

"Someone or no one?" Max pressed.

"She was in our Party a long time ago. She moved away." Mike lied.

"She was a mage. And you Tara?" Max questioned. "What can you do? Magic tricks?"

Tara didn't respond. She thought it best not to.

Max got onto her skateboard.

"Well, I could be your guys's zoomer." Max spoke.

"That's not even a real thing." Mike reminded her.

"It could be!" Max said before going in a circle on her skateboard. "See? Zoomer."

"Mind blowing." Mike said sarcastically.

Tara smiled at Max.

"Come on, you know you're impressed." Max said with a smile.

"Yes." Tara responded.

"I don't see any tricks. You're just going around in a circle." Mike pointed out.

"If it's so easy, you try it." Max spoke.

"I can't." Mike said. "I don't know how."

"I could teach you." Max said.

"Could you teach me?" Tara asked. "One day."

"Definitely!" Max responded. "You're Will's sister right? I'll come over one day and I'll turn you into a skateboarding pro in no time. You can't be better than me of course."

Tara felt her cheeks heating up as her smile widened.

"You're making me dizzy." Mike blurted out. "Please just stop."

"I'll stop when I can join your Party." Max replied. "It's a simple question. Am I in or out?"

"Please." Tara said to Mike with her brown puppy dog eyes.

Max suddenly lost her footing on the board and fell to the ground.

She yelped as she hit her back.

Tara rushed over to her side.

"Are you okay?" Tara asked with caring eyes.

"Yeah, I think so." Max replied as she stood herself up.

"What happened?" Mike asked Max.

"I don't know," Max replied. "It was like a magnet or something pulling on my board. I know that sounds crazy."

Mike shot Tara a look.

Tara shook her head in response. Her nose wasn't bleeding, nor would she do anything to hurt someone who'd done nothing to her.

Mike and Tara rushed out through the swinging doors, glancing around for any sign of her.

FOUR

"**W**ill!" Dustin yelled out for Will. He was missing.

"Dustin! Tara!" Joyce called out as she approached. "What's going on? Tara, where's your brother?"

Lucas rushed through the swinging doors.

"The field!" He exclaimed through panting.

They ran out onto the field, to find Mike shaking Will's shoulders.

"I just found him like this!" Mike rambled through his words to everyone. "I think he's having another episode!"

Max rubbed the back of her neck nervously.

"Will!" Joyce yelled out as she shook him. "Sweetie, wake up! It's Mom!"

It was a risk with Max around, but Tara grabbed Will's cold hand and closed her eyes.

She went into his mind.

The first thing she noticed, the world around her was all dark and cloudy.

Then, she saw Will.

A big shadow monster, like he had described, was with him.

It went into him, into his body, his mouth, everything.

Tara's eyes went a faint red of anger.

"Get away!" Tara yelled as she stuck out her hand.

It was taking her strength and energy, but she didn't stop.

She managed to throw the monster off Will.

They both woke up, in the real world.

Will let out a heavy gasp for air.

Tara fell backwards and Max caught her, confused as ever.

Tara was left feeling awfully drained of energy, but she'd do it again in a heartbeat.

Joyce helped walk Tara and Will over to the car and they got in.

"...I can't remember." Will lied to Joyce.

"I need you to try." Joyce told him.

"I-I was on the field and then it all just went blank and then you were there." Will stammered through his lie.

"Will, I need you to tell me the truth." Joyce asked him.

"I-I am." Will stuttered.

Joyce pulled out a picture she drew.

"This shape, I saw it on the video tape from Halloween night. It's the same shape as your drawing." She told Will. "These episodes that you're having, I think Dr. Owens is wrong. I think they're real. But I can't help you if I don't know what's going on. So you have to talk to me, please. Did you see this thing again on the field?"

"Yes." Tara responded for him in case he lied.

"What is it?" Joyce asked.

"I don't know." Will said, his voice cracking as tears filled his eyes. "It's almost more like a feeling."

"Like, the one you had that night at the Arcade?" Joyce asked him for clarification.

Will nodded, a tear rolling down his cheek.

"What does it want?" Joyce asked.

"To kill. To hurt Will." Tara replied as much as she could figure out.

Will slightly nodded.

"It came for me and- I tried. I tried to make it go away. But it got me, Mom." Will said as more tears ran down his cheeks. "I felt it everywhere. I-I still feel it. I just want this to be over."

Joyce pulled him in for a comforting hug.

"It's okay, Shhh..."

The next day, Joyce let Tara stay home along with Will.

"Why can't I go?" Tara asked. She wanted to see her friends, and Max too.

"Because this isn't normal. We need you. Will needs you." Joyce explained to her as she dialed Hopper's phone number.

Hopper pulled up at the Byer's residence and entered the house.

The house was freezing cold, as Will told Joyce that's what the monster wanted.

Tara wrapped herself up in one of Mike's hoodies, along with a blanket.

"Hello?" Hopper called out.

Tara's eyebrow raised as she recognized his voice.

"Where the hell have you been?" Joyce whispered to Hopper.

"I overslept," Hopper admitted. "What the hell's going on? It's freezing."

Joyce and Hopper entered Will's bedroom, where Tara and Will sat.

Once Hopper's eyes laid on Tara, he was confused.

His gaze went from Tara to Joyce and Will. Tara, to Joyce and Will.

Hopper then let out a scoff of realization. "Of course..."

"Hi." Tara said innocently.

"So this thing, this shadow thing. You told your mom it likes it like this. It likes it cold?" Hopper asked Will.

"Yeah." Will replied.

"How do you know that?" Hopper asked Will.

"I just know." Will said.

"Does he talk to you?" Hopper asked.

"No it's like, I don't have to think. I just know things now. Things I never did before," Will explained.

"And, what else do you know?" Hopper asked Will.

"It's hard to explain. It's like old memories in the back of my head, only they're not my memories." Will explained. "I mean, I don't think their old memories at all. They're now memories, happening all at once, now."

"Can you describe these now memories?" Hopper asked Will, his tone gentle and patient.

"I don't know- it's hard to explain," Will stumbled over his words.

"I know it's hard but can you just try?" Joyce asked Will.

"It's like, they're growing and spreading... killing." Will explained through tears.

Tara held his hand comfortingly.

"The memories?" Joyce asked.

"I don't know, I'm sorry," Will said as he cried into Joyce's shoulder.

Joyce suddenly had an idea.

"Hey, what if you didn't have to use words?" She asked him.

Will grabbed a couple pens and started frantically drawing down on the paper.

FIVE

A couple hours later, Hopper left and Mike came over.

"It's like I feel what the Shadow Monster's feeling. See what he's seeing." Will explained.

"Like in the Upside Down?" Mike asked.

"Some of him is there. But some of him is here too." Will said.

"Here in this house?" Mike asked.

"In this house and," Will paused as he began to tremble. "In me. It's like he's reaching into Hawkins more and more. And the more he spreads, the more connected to him I feel."

"And the more you see these now memories." Mike added.

"At first I just felt it at the back of my head," Will said. "I didn't even really know it was there. It's like when you have a dream and you can't remember it unless you think really hard. It was like that. But now I remember."

"Maybe that's good." Mike spoke softly.

"Good?" Will asked.

"Just think about it Will. You're like a spy now. A super spy," Mike explained. "Spying on the shadow monster. If you know what he's seeing and feeling, maybe that's how we can stop him. Maybe all of this is happening for a reason."

"What if he figures out we're spying on him?" Will asked with worry. "What if he spies back?"

"I'll kill him." Tara said with no hesitation.

The next morning, Will woke up with a start. He gasped for air.

Mike shot up, concerned for his best friend.

"Will, what's wrong?" He asked.

The dynamic trio went up to Joyce, who was surrounded by drawings.

"Mom," Will began. "I saw him."

"Saw who, baby?" Joyce asked.

"Hopper. I think he's in trouble. I think he's going to die." Will revealed.

Joyce's eyes widened.

"I think I wanna go to Dustin's." Tara decided.

"You sure, honey?" Joyce asked.

Tara nodded.

"Be careful." Joyce said as Tara headed out the door.

Tara went over to Dustin's house just as his mom left.

She had tears in her eyes but was faintly smiling.

"Oh, you've come to see Dustin?" She asked.

"Yes." Tara replied.

"Come in." She said before trailing away.

Tara hummed to herself as she entered Dustin's house.

Dustin was wearing an unusual outfit, Tara couldn't even BEGIN to describe.

"Tara?" Dustin asked with confusion. "Why're you here?"

"I wanted to see y-" Tara paused as she noticed the meat on his carpet.

"We have to run, okay? Dart's grown again." Dustin explained quickly as he slowly slid open his bedroom door.

He grabbed Tara's wrist and pulled her along as he ran through his house.

"Oh my god, oh my god," Dustin repeated nervously as they ran outside. "Shit shit."

He pulled the both of them into his shed and quickly closed the door.

Tara felt a little trapped but she had the closest bond with Will and Dustin out of the Party, so she felt safe with Dustin.

"Come on, I know you're hungry," Dustin murmured about Dart.

Dart ran out of Dustin's house and continued to chomp down meat.

Dart turned around and stared at the duo straight in the face.

Dustin and Tara quickly pressed their backs against the wall of the shed, hiding.

Tara opened the shed door with her mind, much to Dustin's panic.

She tilted her head to the side, and Dart got thrown into the basement.

Dustin quickly scrambled over and shut the basement door.

"I'm sorry," Dustin repeated in guilt. "You ate my cat."

"Guys, this is Dustin," Dustin spoke into the walkie while digging up his beloved dead cat. "This is a code red. I repeat, a code red!"

"Could you please shut up?" Erica, Lucas's little sister responded.

"Erica? Is Lucas there?" Dustin frantically asked her.

"Don't know. Don't care." Erica sassily responded.

"I-Is he with Mike?" Dustin stumbled over his words.

"Like I said, I don't know and I don't care." Erica repeated herself.

"Please tell him it's super important. Please tell him that I have a code-" Dustin began.

"Code red?" Erica asked.

A grin spread across Dustin's face.

"Yes." Tara said.

"I got a code for ya'll instead. It's called Code Shut Your Mouth." Erica snapped back before turning the walkie off.

Dustin let out a long sigh.

"C'mon," He said.

"Where are we going?" Tara asked him.

"Follow me and you'll know." Dustin replied.

And they took off, heading in the direction of the Wheelers.

Tara's eyes widened when they got to the Wheelers.

"Dustin-" Tara started, trying to tell Dustin that Mike was at her house.

"Shh," He said as he rang the doorbell.

Ted Wheeler opened the front door.

"Your line has been busy for over two hours, Mr. Wheeler." Dustin said. "Do you realize this?"

"Oh I realize." Ted replied un-amused.

"Is Mike home?" Dustin asked.

"No." Ted replied.

"No? Where the hell is he?" Dustin asked.

"My house." Tara said.

"Nancy. What about Nancy?" Dustin asked.

"Karen, where's Nancy?" Ted yelled over to Karen.

"Ally!" Karen yelled back.

"Ally's." Ted replied. "Our children don't live here anymore. You didn't know that?"

"Seriously?" Dustin asked unimpressed.

"Am I done here?" Ted asked impatiently.

"Son of a bitch; You really are no help at all, you know that?" Dustin cursed under his breath.

"Mouthbreather." Tara added as they walked off.

"Language!" Ted scolded them.

At that time, Steve pulled up by the Wheelers. He had a bouquet of flowers in his hand.

"I was thinking, I love you. I'm sorry," Steve muttered to himself. "I'm sorry? What the hell am I sorry for?"

"Steve." Dustin spoke as Steve stopped and waited in place for the dynamic duo.

"Are those for Mr. or Mrs. Wheeler?" Dustin asked Steve.

"No?" Steve responded confused.

"Good." Dustin snatched the flowers.

"What the hell-" Steve exclaimed in annoyance.

"Nancy isn't home," Dustin told him.

"Where is she?" Steve asked.

"Doesn't matter. We have bigger problems than your love life," Dustin insulted as he opened up the car door. "Do you still have that bat?"

"What bat?" Steve asked.

"The one with the nails." Dustin narrowed it down.

"Why?" Steve asked.

"I'll explain it on the way." Dustin said.

Tara got in the passenger seat.

"Now?" Steve asked, unaware he just got himself into a full-time job of babysitting.

"Now!" Dustin confirmed.

SIX

S teve lifted up the boot of his car and pulled out his iconic baseball bat.

The three stood right by the basement where Dart was in.

"I don't hear shit." Steve muttered in disbelief.

"He's in there." Dustin assured him.

"Promise." Tara added.

"Yeah, I don't do pinky finger promises. I swear if this is some sort of Halloween prank, you're dead." Steve threatened to which Tara glared at him for.

"It's not a prank." Dustin said.

Steve opened up the door of the basement.

"I'll stay up here in case he tries to... escape." Dustin said as Tara backed up with him.

Steve sighed before entering the basement.

"Steve?" Dustin called nervously.

Steve flashed the flashlight up at their faces.

Tara winced in surprise.

"Get down here." Steve said.

Dustin and Tara made their way down to the basement. To their surprise, Dart was gone.

On the end of Steve's baseball bat, was Dart's skin. He had grew again.

"Oh, shit!" Dustin cursed.

Dart had also broke a hole in the wall and escaped through there.

"No way," Dustin mumbled in surprise.

The next morning, Dustin and Tara were still with Steve.

"Dustin!" Lucas frantically said from the walkie. "This is Lucas. Do you copy? Dustin?"

"Well well well, look who it is." Dustin teased with an annoyed smirk.

"Sorry man. My stupid sister turned it off." Lucas explained.

"While you were having sister problems, Dart grew again, he escaped and I'm pretty sure he's a baby Demogorgon." Dustin said.

"Wait. What?" Lucas asked.

"I'll explain later. Meet me, Tara and Steve at the old junkyard." Dustin said. "And bring your binoculars and wrist rocket."

"Steve? Steve Harrington?" Lucas exclaimed in shock.

"Just be there stat! Over and out." Dustin said.

It took a while but they made it to the junkyard.

"Oh yeah. This'll do." Steve said with a proud smile.

"I said medium well!" Lucas yelled at them.

The three looked over and saw Lucas, alongside him was Max.

Tara waved at them with a smile.

"Who's that?" Steve asked.

"Max." Tara explained. "Zoomer."

"Uh- Okay." Steve furrowed his eyebrows in confusion but simply shook it off.

"You told her?" Dustin exclaimed in shock.

"So what?" Lucas shrugged. "You wanted to tell her too."

"Yeah but I didn't. We all agreed not to tell her and to look for Dart." Dustin reminded him.

"Who you conveniently found." Lucas said.

Tara opened her mouth to say something but Dustin held his hand over her mouth, so she wouldn't spill about Dart.

"Are you suggesting that I'm lying?" Dustin asked.

"I'm saying you have a creepy little bond with him." Lucas explained.

"Yeah, that was before he turned into a Demogorgon!" Dustin defended.

"And you haven't heard from Mike?" Lucas asked.

"No." The duo replied.

"Or Will?"

"No."

"Hopper?"

"No!" Dustin said, raising his voice. "No one is around. Why do you think we're with Steve Harrington? Something's--"

"Wrong. I agree." Lucas agreed before glancing over at Max. "Which is why we need as much help as we can get."

Max was struggling to lift up a heavy object by the bus. The same bus El, Mike, Tara, Dustin and Lucas hid in while the bad men were on the lookout for them.

Tara rose to her feet and approached Max.

"Help?" Tara asked her.

"Yeah, sure." Max said with a smile.

Tara moved the objects Max was struggling with, with her mind over to the bus.

Max stared in amazement.

"Lucas really wasn't lying." Max said in shock. "About everything."

"Friends don't lie." Tara responded.

"Yeah, he said that." Max said with a laugh. "So, what else can you do? With your powers?"

"Dustin says I can..." Tara paused as she focused on her words. "Teleport and telepathy too."

"Holy shit, that's insane!" Max giggled in awe.

"Hey! Dickheads! How come the only ones helping me out are this random girl and baldy?" Steve yelled to Dustin and Steve.

"She's not bald anymo-" Dustin started but Steve glared at him.

After what felt like an eternity, they had the bus ready.

Inside the bus, Steve flicked around with his lighter.

"So you really fought one of these things before?" Max asked as Tara sat with her.

Steve nodded.

"And you're like totally, 100% sure it wasn't a bear?" Max asked.

"Shit, don't be an idiot okay? It wasn't a bear." Dustin snapped at her. "Why are you even here if you don't believe us? I mean, wasn't seeing Tara use her powers enough for your tiny brain? Just go home."

Tara glared at him.

"Jeez, someone's cranky. Past your bedtime?" Max insulted back as she climbed up the ladder.

Tara joined her and they sat on top of the bus roof together.

"It's kinda awesome." Max started off as she gazed off at the fog. "The fog. Looks like the ocean."

"Ocean?" Tara asked.

"Where I lived, California. Had oceans. But it also had my dad; he's still there." Max said, the last bit accidentally slipping out.

"Why?" Tara asked.

"It's this legal term called divorce." Max joked sarcastically before realizing Tara was clueless.

"When two married people don't love each other anymore, they separate." Max explained.

Tara nodded in understanding.

"My mom and my stepdad, they wanted a fresh start away from him. As if he was the problem, which is total bull. And things are just worse now." Max said to Tara.

Tara listened. She listened to every last word.

"My stepbrother's always been a dick but now he's just angry all the time and," Max paused to take a deep breath in. "Well, he can't take it out on my mom so..."

"Hurts you?" Tara asked. She knew full well what Max meant.

"I don't even know why I'm telling you this." Max said, feeling embarrassed that she'd opened up.

"It's just, I know that I can be a jerk like him sometimes, and I do not want to be like him. Ever." Max continued.

"I guess I'm angry too and I'm sorry." Max apologized.

Tara held Max's hand in hers.

"Friend's don't lie; You're nothing like him. Nothing," Tara said, trying to comfort Max. "It's okay."

Max quickly wiped her tearing up eyes.

"You think so?" Max asked.

"Yes." Tara confirmed. "You're better. You're pretty and cool."

Max smiled, gazing off into Tara's eyes.

"I'll protect you from him." Tara promised her. "I promise. And friend's don't lie."

A sudden screech in the distance alerted the two girls.

Lucas quickly crawled up the ladder and onto the top of the bus, wearing his binoculars.

In the fog, Lucas could make out one Demogorgon.

"I've got eyes! Ten o'clock!" Lucas yelled down to Steve and Dustin.

"Wait. You're sure that's not a dog?" Max asked.

Tara shook her head no.

And then, the plans changed.

Steve exited the bus slowly, baseball bat in hand.

He whistled to get the Demogorgon's attention.

"Come on, buddy. Dinner time; human tastes better than cat. I promise." Steve called out.

Tara and Max quickly climbed down the ladder.

"He's insane." Max said in shock.

"He's cool." Tara said.

"He's awesome." Dustin added with a grin of amazement.

Before long, Demogorgons began to circle Steve.

Tara flung open the bus door and threw a Demogorgon away from reach of Steve with her mind.

Steve ran for the bus, but more Demogorgons chased after him.

Tara flung them back with her mind and Steve got inside the bus safely.

Tara fell backwards next to Max.

"Are they rabid or something?" Max asked as the Demogorgons rammed themselves against the door.

"They can't get in!" Lucas yelled to reassure himself.

Dustin frantically rushed over to grab the walkie.

He turned it on.

"Is anyone there? Mike? Will? God?" Dustin spoke rather quickly. "We are at the old junkyard and we are going to die!"

Max slowly raised her head up, only to be met with a pair of eyes.

A pair of Demogorgon eyes, nonetheless.

Max screamed aloud fearfully.

Tara dragged Max over to her with her mind, her nose bleeding.

"Thanks." Max said while her heart was racing.

The Demogorgons suddenly took off, heading somewhere.

Tara did feel drained but it was worth it to save Steve and Max.

Steve slowly exited the bus, cautiously and hesitantly.

"What happened?" Lucas asked in disbelief.

"They're going somewhere." Steve replied.

SEVEN

"You're positive that was Dart?" Lucas asked Dustin for clarification.

"Yes. He had the same exact yellow pattern on his butt." Dustin replied.

"But he was tiny two days ago." Max reminded him bemusedly.

"Well, he's molted three times already." Dustin explained. "Shed his skin to make room for growth like hornworms."

"When's he gonna molt again?" Max asked.

"It's gotta be soon. When he does, he'll be fully grown or close to it." Dustin replied. "And so will his friends."

"Yeah and he's gonna eat a lot more than just cats." Steve said, much to Dustin's dismay.

"Wait, a cat? Dart ate a cat?" Lucas asked in shock.

"No." Dustin lied."

"What are you talking about? He ate Mews." Steve said.

"Who's Mews?" Max asked.

"Dustin's cat." Steve and Tara said in unison.

"Steve! Tara!" Dustin yelled in dismay.

"I knew it!" Lucas exclaimed while shoving Dustin. "You kept him!"

"No- He missed me. He wanted to come home." Dustin admitted.

"Bullshit!" Lucas exclaimed in anger.

"I didn't know he was a Demogorgon, okay?!" Dustin defended.

"Oh, so now you admit it?" Lucas snapped back.

"Guys, who cares? We have to go." Max said.

"I care! You put the Party in jeopardy!" Lucas said to Dustin. "You broke the rule of law!"

"So did you!" Dustin yelled. "You told a stranger the truth."

Max stepped forwards.

"A stranger?" She asked in disbelief.

"You wanted to tell her too!" Lucas reminded him.

"Yeah but I didn't." Dustin replied. "We both broke the rule of law. So we're even."

"No! We're not even; don't even try that!" Lucas said. "Your stupid pet could've had us for dinner!"

"That was not my fault!" Dustin defended.

"Guys?" Steve called out but they all ignored him.

"He wasn't going to eat us." Dustin added.

"Oh, so he was just crawling to come say hello?" Lucas asked sarcastically.

"Guys!" Steve yelled, finally getting their attention.

They all ran towards a faint screeching sound.

"No- Guys, why are you headed towards the sound?" Max asked. "Hello?"

Max hesitantly ran after them.

Lucas put his binoculars back on.

"It's the lab. They were going back home." Lucas said.

Tara tensed up as they were somewhat close to the Lab; a place she did not ever want to see again.

They heard voices in the distance so they decided to check it out.

They squinted their eyes at the figures, only to find Nancy and Jonthan.

"Steve?" Nancy and Jonathan both asked in shock.

"Nancy?" Steve asked in surprise.

"Jonathan!" Tara said as Jonathan pulled her in for a hug. "You okay?"

Tara nodded.

"What are you doing here?" Nancy asked Steve.

"What are you doing here?" He asked her.

"We're looking for Mike and Will." Nancy replied.

"They're not in there, are they?" Dustin asked nervously.

"We're not sure." Nancy replied.

"Why?" Jonathan asked.

"The power's back." Nancy suddenly said as the Lab lights all came on abruptly.

"Guys?" Max called as a car suddenly drove past.

Tara dragged Max back just in time with her mind.

"You have to stop doing that," Max chuckled.

Hopper's car pulled up right by them.

"Let's go." He said as they all hopped inside.

Tara glanced at Joyce and noticed she was crying.

"You're okay?" Tara asked.

Joyce took a deep breath in as more tears rolled down her cheek.

"Oh, honey." She whispered, her voice cracking. "Bob is-"

"Bob's gone." Mike said for Joyce. "The Demogorgon killed him."

Tara felt tears threatening to fall. She was beginning to like Bob.

Tara fought back tears as she gazed off at the window of the car.

"Did you guys know that Bob was the original founder of Hawkins AV?" Mike asked them.

"Really?" Dustin asked.

"He petitioned the school to start it and everything. Then he had a fundraiser for equipment. Mr. Clarke learned everything from him." Mike said. "Pretty awesome, right?"

"Yes." Tara responded, her hand in Max's.

"We can't let him die in vain." Mike said.

"What do you want to do, Mike? The chief's right on this; we can't stop those Demo Dogs on our own." Dustin replied.

"Demo Dogs?" Max and Tara asked in unison.

"Demogorgon dogs." Dustin narrowed it down for them. "Demo Dogs. It's like a compound. A play on words--"

"Okay." Max cut him off before he could continue.

"I mean, when it was just Dart maybe..." Dustin trailed off.

"But there's an army now." Lucas said.

"Precisely." Dustin agreed.

"His army." Mike realized with wide eyes. "Maybe if we can stop him, we can stop his army too!"

"The shadow monster." Dustin mumbled.

"It got Will that day on the field. The Doctors said it was like a virus, it infected him." Mike explained further.

"And so this virus, its connecting him to the tunnels?" Max questioned.

"To the tunnels, monsters, the Upside Down, everything." Mike replied.

"Woah, slow down." Steve told him.

"Okay so, the shadow monster's inside everything. And if the vines feel something like pain, then so does Will." Mike explained.

"And so does Dart." Lucas added.

"Yeah. Like what Mr. Clarke taught us. The hive mind." Mike said.

"Hive mind?" Tara and Steve asked in unison.

"A collective consciousness. It's a super organism." Dustin explained.

"And this is the thing that controls everything. It's the brain," Mike said while grabbing a drawing of the shadow monster.

"Like the mind flayer." Dustin realized.

Lucas snapped his fingers in realization.

After explaining to everyone what The Mind Flayer was, Hopper let out a scoff.

"What the hell are we doing here?" He scoffed.

"I thought we were waiting for your military backup!" Mike exclaimed. "Even if they come, how are they gonna stop this? You can't just shoot this with guns!"

"You don't know that! We don't know anything!" Hopper yelled back.

"We know it's already killed everybody in that Lab!" Mike responded.

"And we know the monsters are gonna molt again." Lucas added.

"And we know that it's only a matter of time before those tunnels reach this town." Dustin added as well.

"They're right." Joyce said as she walked in the room. "We have to kill it. I want to kill it."

"Me too. But how do we do that?" Hopper asked. "We don't exactly know what we're dealing with here."

"No. But he does." Mike realized while referring to Will. "If anyone knows how to destroy this thing, it's Will. He's connected to it; he'll know its weakness."

"I thought we couldn't trust him anymore; that he's a spy for the Mind flayer now." Max said.

"He can't spy if he doesn't know where he is." Mike replied.

They'd been trying to get Will to talk to them, but Will was gone. Just an empty shell of him.

That was until Hopper walked over to the others.

"What happened?" Dustin asked.

Hopper wrote something down on a piece of paper.

"I think he's talking, just not with words." Hopper explained.

"What is that?" Steve asked as the others recognized it as Morse code.

"Morse code." The others replied.

"H E R E." Hopper translated.

"Will's still in there. He's talking to us." Hopper said.

The next hour consisted of them trying to figure out what Will was saying to them.

"Close Gate." They finally translated.

Just then, the house phone rang.

But Nancy was quick to yank it off the wall.

They heard a faint screeching sound.

"That's not good." Dustin muttered.

"They're coming!" Jonathan said.

"Hey! Get away from the windows!" Hopper yelled to the kids who backed away from the window.

"Do you know how to use this?" He asked Jonathan who shook his head.

"I can." Nancy replied.

Hopper handed her the gun.

Tara was more than ready to fight the Demo Dogs.

Lucas held out his wrist rocket, aiming at the windows while Mike grabbed a candle holder for protection.

The screeching suddenly stopped.

The Demo dog flew through the window, only to land lifeless at Hopper's feet.

"Holy shit." Dustin cursed.

"Did you?" Mike asked Tara, but she shook her head.

Her nose wasn't bleeding. Not one drop.

"Is it dead?" Max asked.

Hopper gently kicked the Demo Dog with his foot.

The Demo Dog remained dead.

The front door unlocked with a click.

The door slowly opened by itself.

A girl walked through the door.

She had dark black short hair, the same length as Tara's. She was dressed up in a punk outfit.

Eleven.

EIGHT

"Eleven," Mike breathed out.

El threw her arms around him, pulling him in for a tight embrace.

"Is that..." Max asked in awe.

Lucas and Dustin nodded.

"I never gave up on you. I called you every night for--" Mike told her with a smile.

"353 days." El replied. "I heard."

"Why didn't you tell me you were there?" Mike asked her. "That you were okay?"

"Because I wouldn't let her." Hopper replied as he approached them.

"What the hell is this? Where've you been?" Hopper asked as he hugged El.

Mike's eyes widened in anger.

"You've been hiding her. You've been hiding her this whole time!" He angrily shoved Hopper. "Would you've done this to Tara as well?! You-"

"Hey!" Hopper grabbed Mike's arm. "Let's talk. Alone."

Hopper pulled Mike over to a separate room to talk.

El inhaled deeply.

"Hi." Tara said as her eyes welled with tears.

They embraced one another, hugging tightly.

A tear rolled down Tara's cheek. This whole time, all she needed was her sister.

When they finally pulled apart, El hugged Lucas and Dustin.

Then, Max approached her.

"Hey, I'm Max." Max said as she extended her hand out. "I've heard a lot about you."

El glared at her before brushing past her hand.

"You and Tara opened this gate before, right?" Joyce asked El.

El nodded.

"Do you think, if we got you both back there, that you could close it?" Joyce asked El as Tara walked over.

"Yes." Tara immediately replied.

"It's not like it was before. It's grown; a lot. And that's considering we can even get in there. That place is crawling with those dogs." Hopper explained.

Tara's hand was in Max's.

"Demo Dogs." Dustin corrected.

"I'm sorry, what?" Hopper asked.

"I said, Demo Dogs. Like Demogorgon and dogs. You put them together, it sounds pretty badass-"Dustin explained.

"How is this important right now?" Hopper asked.

"It's not, I'm sorry." Dustin apologized.

"I can do it." El said confidently.

"You're not hearing me-" Hopper tried to tell her.

"I'm hearing you." El repeated.

"We can do it." Tara added.

"Even if they can, there's still another problem." Mike said. "If the brain dies the body dies."

"I thought that was the whole point." Max said.

"It is, but if we're really right about this, I mean, if El and Tara close the gate and kill the mind flayer's army..." Mike trailed off.

"Will's a part of that army." Lucas mumbled.

"Closing the gate would kill him." Mike said.

"He likes it cold." Joyce mumbled before rushing to close the windows. "We keep giving it what it wants!"

"If this is a virus and Will is the host then..." Nancy's voice trailed off as she looked down at Will's unconscious body.

"Then we need to make the host uninhabitable." Jonathan finished her sentence.

"So if he likes it cold..." Nancy started.

"We need to burn it out of him." Joyce growled in determination.

"We have to do it somewhere he doesn't know this time." Mike said.

"Yeah, somewhere far away." Dustin added.

Hopper got in his truck, as Joyce, Jonathan and Will drove off.

He waited for El and Tara to say their goodbyes.

El was saying goodbye to Mike, while Tara was with Max.

"Be careful, okay?" Max told Tara.

Tara nodded.

"I mean, you're totally badass and I believe you'll kick the Mind Flayer's ass, but be careful." Max said with a smile.

"El, Tara, come on. Let's go. It's time." Hopper said impatiently just as El was leaning into Mike's lips.

The two sisters hopped into his truck and he began to drive off.

"So, Tara," Hopper started off. "You've been living with Joyce?"

Tara nodded with a hum.

"She's let you go out places? I guess?" Hopper asked awkwardly, trying to make conversation with her.

"Yes." Tara responded.

El's eye slightly twitched with jealousy. This past year, all she wanted was to be with Mike. Tara got to.

"It's nice to know that you haven't changed." Hopper commented, referring to El's new look.

El said nothing.

"So, we're just not gonna talk about it?" Hopper asked El.

"About what?" El asked coldly.

"Oh, I don't know; I'm just curious why all of a sudden you look like some kind of MTV punk." Hopper joked.

El turned her head away in annoyance and sadness.

"I'm not mad, kid. I just wanna know where you've been." Hopper said, his tone softer now.

"To see Mama." El admitted.

Hopper went as pale as a ghost.

"Okay," He nervously started. "How'd you get there?"

"A big truck." El replied.

Hopper's eyes widened.

"Who's truck was it?" He asked.

"A nice man's." El replied casually.

"Okay so let me just get this straight in my head. A nice man in a big truck drove you to your mama's and then what? Your aunt becky gave you those clothes and that makeup?" Hopper asked in confusion and fear.

"I-I shouldn't have left." El stammered.

"No this isn't on you kid. I should've been there. I should never have lied to you about your mom or about when you could leave. There's a lot of things I shouldn't have done." Hopper apologized.

"Sometimes I feel like I'm some kind of black hole." Hopper added with a sad expression.

"A black hole?" El and Tara asked.

"Yeah it's this thing in Outer space. It sucks everything towards it and destroys it." Hopper explained.

"Sarah had a picture book about outer space; she loved it." Hopper added with a sad sniffle.

"Who's Sarah?" El and Tara asked in unison.

"Sarah's my little girl." Hopper replied.

"Where is she?" El asked.

"That's kind of the thing, kid. She left us." Hopper said.

"Gone?" El asked as a tear rolled down her cheek.

"Yeah, the black hole. It got her." Hopper said, although his words had a hidden meaning.

Tara touched his shoulder comfortingly, as if she understood what he meant.

Hopper slightly smiled at Tara, before continuing.

"And somehow, I've just been scared that it would take you too. I think that's why I get so-" Hopper paused to think of the correct way to word his sentence.

"Stupid?" El asked.

Tara fought back a giggle.

El reached for his hand, and took his in her own.

"I've been stupid too," El said.

"I guess we broke our rule." Hopper joked before glancing at her. "I don't hate it by the way. This whole look. It's kinda cool."

"Bitching." El said.

"Okay. Sure." Hopper said in a slightly confused manner.

"No. It's badass." Tara said. That was a word she learnt from Max. She hadn't the faintest idea what it meant, but hopefully it meant something good.

"You two sure are sisters." Hopper joked.

It wasn't long before they arrived at their destination.

They pulled up by the Lab.

The three got out of the car together.

Tara froze; her eyes wide with fright as she looked up at the familiar lab in front of her.

Memories flashed inside her head; every brutal punishment Papa did to her, everything.

"I-I can't..." Tara whispered while taking a step back.

El gently reached for Tara's hand with a reassuring look.

"I don't want to either but we have to." El said.

"All right, you guys let me do the heavy lifting up front." Hopper instructed as he carried a large gun. "Save your strength til we're below."

He noticed the girls expressions.

"You okay?" He asked.

Tara didn't respond as her and El began walking forward to the source of their trauma.

They walked down many staircases, but one caught their attention.

It was covered in blood.

Hopper cautiously approached only to find Dr. Owens, bleeding out.

"Oh shit." He whispered as he knelt down beside Dr. Owens.

Dr. Owen's leg was bleeding quite badly.

El and Tara came into view.

"Oh yeah, I've been meaning to tell you," Hopper said while keeping pressure on Dr. Owen's wound. "That's Eleven and Twelve-"

"I know that girl. Tara." Dr. Owens said quietly from the pain.

"Oh that's good. You're already acquainted! But Eleven's been staying with me for about a year and her and Tara are about to save our asses." Hopper said proudly.

They made it to the Gate.

El and Tara put their hand out, starting to close the opened gate.

It wasn't long before they felt drained but they couldn't stop now.

They began bleeding from their ears too.

The gate eventually closed.

Tara collapsed to the ground, low on energy.

She eyelids fluttered as she took a deep breath.

It was all over now.

NINE

One month had passed, and it was the night of the Snowball.

Joyce helped Tara get dolled up to the best of their abilities.

"You guys have a fun night." Joyce said while tears formed in her eyes with a smile.

"We will!" Will said while practically dragging Tara by the hand into the school.

Loud dance music filled their ears, and the smell of tasty snacks satisfied their smells.

Will pushed open the swinging doors and continued dragging Tara over to their friends.

"Byers!" Lucas exclaimed with a grin.

Max shot Tara a smile.

Tara, of course, shot one back.

Mike's jaw suddenly dropped as somebody walked into the gymnasium.

Dustin approached his group of friends. He was dressed up nicely, and his hair was done for tonight.

"Holy shit, what happened to you?" Mike asked.

"What do you mean, what happened?" Dustin asked nervously.

"What?" Mike asked with a grin.

"Your hair." Max commented.

"Is there a bird nesting in there?" Lucas joked.

"Not badass." Tara said, eyeing Dustin's hair.

"Nice one." Max chuckled to her.

"Assholes." Dustin said with a glare. "I worked hard."

A slow romantic song came on.

"Max." Tara called as she turned to the redhead.

Max turned around.

"Could we- I mean? Snowball?" Tara asked, trying to find the correct words. "Dance?"

Max smiled. "You're asking me to dance?"

"Yes." Tara responded.

Max tilted her head to the side, as if to think things over before a grin spread across her face.

"Come on." She said as she led Tara to the dance floor.

Tara wrapped her arms around Max, as Max was a bit taller.

Max placed her hands onto Tara's waist, sending a shock of butterflies into Tara's stomach.

Tara kept her gaze on Max's, getting lost in her ocean blue eyes. The same color as water, the sky and butterflies. Such pretty things. Like Max.

"Pretty." Tara commented.

"Like you can talk." Max responded as her cheeks grew pink. "You're absolutely stunning. Gorgeous."

Tara's heart fluttered at Max's compliments.

Max leaned in and pressed her lips against Tara's.

Max pulled apart, admiring Tara's features.

"I know this is kind of the things you do with a boy, your boyfriend, or a boy you like," Max paused before continuing. "And I don't know if you know this but, I like you."

Tara's eyes slightly widened.

"I like you a lot, Tara. And not just your powers. I like you in general." Max continued. "I was happy you wanted to dance with me because I wanted to dance with you. But I guess I was too afraid too. I didn't want you to turn me down or-"

"I like you too." Tara said.

Max's eyes lit up.

"So- what does this make us?" She asked.

"Girlfriends." Tara confirmed.

Max smiled before pressing her lips onto the girl's once more.

TEN

It was the start of summer, and Tara couldn't be thrilled!

Granted, Dustin was at summer camp but she was still having the time of her life with her friends.

Will, Lucas, Max and Tara stood next to one another waiting for Mike of course.

Mike finally pulled up by them, parking his bike.

"You're late!" Lucas complained. "Again."

"Sorry!" Mike apologized.

"We're gonna miss the opening." Will said.

"Yeah if you guys keep whining about it!" Mike responded. "Let's go!"

Lucas mocked Mike much to his dismay.

"Just please stop talking, dude." Mike pleaded.

"Let me guess, you were busy." Lucas said with a smirk.

"Oh yeah, real mature Lucas." Mike said while rolling his eyes.

"Oh El, I wish we could make out forever and never hang out with any of our friends!" Lucas teased.

"Lucas stop." Max told him.

"Will thinks it's funny." Lucas said as Will chuckled.

"Because it is!" Will replied.

"Yeah, it's so funny that I want to spend romantic time with my girlfriend!" Mike exclaimed in frustration.

"Tara's spending romantic time with her girlfriend." Lucas said.

Tara's hand was in Max's.

They rushed down the escalator and past people.

"Hey, watch it!" One lady exclaimed aloud.

"Yeah, watch it nerds!" Erica said.

"Isn't it past your bedtime?" Lucas asked sarcastically.

"Isn't it time you died?" Erica snapped back.

"Psycho." Lucas insulted.

"Buttface." Erica said.

"Mall rat!" Lucas yelled.

"Fart face!" Erica yelled back.

Lucas blew a raspberry at her.

They walked into Scoops Ahoy, where Steve currently worked.

They walked over to the front counter and rang the bell.

Robin stared at them with an empty expression.

"Hey dingus, your children are here!" She yelled out.

Steve pushed open the window.

"Again? Seriously?" He asked.

Mike rang the bell once more.

Steve let them in and they walked down a hall.

"If anybody hears about this--" Steve started with a threat.

"We're dead!" They all cut him off.

They sneak into the movie theater and found a line of seats.

Tara was in the middle of Max and Lucas. Mike and Will sat next to each other.

"See Lucas? We made it." Mike said.

"We still missed the previews." Lucas complained.

"Still made it." Max said.

Will handed out drinks and snacks to everybody just before the movie began to play.

The movie suddenly stopped, the power must've gone out.

Everybody groaned in great annoyance.

"Come on!" Mike and Max groaned out in unison.

But a few minutes later, the power returned.

Tara relaxed in her seat, her hand dipping into the popcorn bowl.

Max's hand dug in the bowl and brushed against Tara's.

They both smiled at each other.

Tara suddenly had an idea and dug through her backpack for a note and a pen.

She began to write.

Wanna sleep over? :)

She showed Max the note with a hopeful expression.

Max nodded with a grin.

Max often slept over at Tara's; she didn't want to scare Tara with Neil or Billy's behavior.

Nor the massive alcohol in the house.

Once they got to Tara's house, Joyce called out.

"Hey! That you guys?" She yelled through the house.

Tara wandered over to find Joyce.

Joyce was sat on the couch with a glass of wine.

"It's okay if Max could sleep the night?" Tara asked Joyce.

Joyce nodded. "It'd be a pleasure!"

"Going to my room." Tara told Joyce as her and Max linked hands.

ELEVEN

Tara and Max sat down at the table for breakfast that morning.

"His reaction will be priceless!" Max giggled.

"What?" Will asked.

"Dustin's. When we surprise him." Max explained. "Thanks for breakfast, Mrs. B!"

Joyce nodded to her with a smile.

Max pulled Tara to her feet.

"C'mon." Max said as their hands entwined.

Once Tara and Max had left, Will frowned.

"Ugh, gross." He commented.

"You're not gonna find it gross when you fall in love." Joyce told him.

"I'm not gonna fall in love." Will sheepishly replied.

The six Party members hid behind a wall in Dustin's home.

El was moving Dustin's toys with her mind, to lure him out into his living room area.

Tara was making him hear voices that weren't there, in his head.

Max quickly wiped Tara's bleeding nose.

"It's just a dream..." Dustin repeated over and over, as he grabbed hair spray.

Tara and El's eyes snapped open and the six slowly approached a fearful Dustin.

Max counted down with her fingers as Lucas held up a sign that read 'Welcome Home!'.

They all blew out party blowers.

Dustin jumped fresh out of his skin and abruptly turned around.

He sprayed whoever was closer with the hair spray.

Unfortunately, it was Lucas.

In Dustin's bedroom, he was showing Mike, Will, El and Tara what he had invented.

"...I would like you to meet... Cerebro." Dustin excitedly said.

Tara's head tilted as she tried to figure it out.

Dustin noticed her lost expression.

"An un-assembled one of a kind battery powered radio tower." Dustin explained in his own way.

"So, it's a ham radio?" Will asked.

"The Cadillac of ham radios." Dustin said with a grin. "This baby carries a crystal clear connection over vast distances. I'm talking North Pole to south. I can talk to my girlfriend whenever and wherever I choose."

Their eyes widened.

"Girlfriend?"

"Wait, so her name is Suzie?" Mike asked.

"Suzie with a z. She's from utah." Dustin replied.

"Girls go to science camp?" Will asked.

"Suzie does; she's a genius." Dustin replied.

"Is she cute?" Mike asked.

"Think Phoebe Cates, only hotter." Dustin said.

"What's going on?" Max asked.

"Going to talk to Dustin's girlfriend." Will replied.

Max and Lucas's eyes widened as they went to chase after the five.

"Aren't we high enough?" Lucas asked as they forced themselves up the hill.

"Cerebro works best at a hundred meters." Dustin said.

"You know, I'm pretty sure people in utah have telephones." Max said.

"Yeah, but Suzie's Mormon." Dustin said.

"Oh shit, she doesn't have electricity?" Lucas asked.

"That's the Amish." Max said.

"What are Mormons?" Will asked.

"Super religious white people." Dustin narrowed it down. "They have electricity and cars but since I'm not Mormon, her parents would never approve."

"It's all very Shakesperean." He added.

"Shakesperean." Max repeated.

"Yeah, like romeo and juliet." Dustin explained. "Star crossed lovers."

"Right." Max said in understanding.

"Hey guys!" Mike yelled.

They turned around.

"This is fun and all but..." Mike trailed off as he pointed down towards his watch.

"I have to go home." El said.

"But we're almost there!" Dustin said.

"Sorry man. Curfew." Mike lied.

"Good luck." El said with a smile.

Mike began to led El away with him.

"Curfew at 4:00?" Dustin frowned in suspicion.

"They're lying." Lucas said.

"It's been like this all summer." Will added.

"It's romantic." Max said.

"It's gross." Will said.

"It's bullshit." Dustin said. "I just got home. Well, their loss right? Suzie awaits! Onwards and upwards!"

Max, Lucas and Tara all groaned in great dismay.

They had finally made it.

Tara felt so hot and thirsty. And her legs felt weak from all that walking.

"I'm so hot." Tara complained.

"Yes, you ar--" Max cut herself off before she finished that sentence. "He re."

She brought a bottle of water out of the backpack and was about to hand it to Tara before Lucas snatched it from her hand.

Lucas began gulping down the water.

Max glared at him.

He wiped his mouth after he finished drinking.

"Did you seriously just drink the rest of our water?" Max asked.

He spit the water back into the bottle.

Tara frowned at him.

Once, they had finished setting Cerebro up, Dustin plopped himself down on the grass.

"Now, are you ready to meet my love?" He asked everyone.

"Yes." Tara replied.

Dustin spoke into his walkie. "Suzie, this is Dustin. Do you copy? Over."

He didn't get a response.

So he continued.

He continued even after the sun had set and it was nightfall.

"...This is Dustin. Over." Dustin continued as the others stared up at the starry night.

Tara was honestly drifting off to sleep, her head on Max's shoulder.

"Suzie-" Dustin began.

"Dustin! Come on; she's not there." Max exclaimed suddenly.

"She's there, alright? She'll pick up!" Dustin responded.

"Maybe Cerebro doesn't work." Will suggested.

"Or maybe Suzie doesn't exist!" Lucas said.

"She exists!" Dustin defended.

"She's a genius AND she's hotter than Phoebe Cates? No girl is that perfect." Lucas said.

"Is that so? Because Tara is sitting right here." Max said, sitting up abruptly.

"You know what I mean-" Lucas began nervously.

"Elaborate." Max said.

"She's not like most girls." Lucas slowly explained.

"Believe me, I know." Max said. "She's better."

Lucas sighed, giving up on explaining.

"Tara is as perfect as I am, and Dustin's obviously lying!" Max stated while standing herself up.

Dustin frowned, seemingly hurt.

"Where are you going?" Dustin asked.

"Home. I'll see you tomorrow, okay?" Max said to Tara with a smile. "My mom will kill me if I'm not home for at least another night."

"Why can't I sleep over?" Tara asked curiously.

"It's... complicated." Max slowly replied.

Lucas got bored too and ended up leaving, so it was just Will, Tara and Dustin now.

"Well, guess it's just us, Byers." Dustin said.

"Um, it's late." Will said as he looked at his watch on his wrist.

"Maybe tomorrow we can play D&D or something fun? Like we used to." Will asked with hopeful eyes.

"Yeah sure." Dustin nodded.

"Welcome home." Will said.

Will and Tara then made their way home.

TWELVE

T ara hummed to herself as she inhaled the cool summer air.

A hand touched her shoulder.

She spun around to find El.

She smiled.

"Hi." El said although she seemed off. "Where are you going?"

"To Max's." Tara replied.

"Can I come?" El hesitantly asked.

They made it to Max's.

She was outside her house, practicing on her skateboard.

It went wrong, and Max tripped off the skateboard.

The skateboard rolled down the street and El stopped it with her foot.

She picked up the board and approached Max.

"Hi." El said before handing over the skateboard.

"Hi?" Max replied, unsure.

"Can we talk?" El asked.

"And then he said he missed me and then he just hung up." El explained to Max in Max's bedroom.

"He's a piece of shit." Max insulted.

"What?" El asked.

"Mike obviously doesn't have jack shit to do today and his nana obviously isn't sick!" Max exclaimed. "I guarantee you, him and Lucas are playing atari right now."

"But friends don't lie." El said.

"Yeah well, boys lie. All the time." Max replied with a glare.

She then sat next to El.

"You're going to stop calling him. You're going to ignore his calls. As far as you're concerned, he doesn't exist." Max told the brunette firmly.

"Doesn't exist?" El asked.

"He treated you like garbage!" Max exclaimed. "You're gonna treat him like garbage. Give him a taste of his own medicine."

"Give him the medicine." El said confidently.

Max nodded proudly.

"And if he doesn't fix this, if he doesn't explain himself, dump his ass." Max told her.

El's eyes widen along with Tara's.

"Come on." Max said as she took El and Tara's hand.

"Where are we going?" El asked.

"To have some fun!" Max replied with a smile. "There's more to life than stupid boys, y'know?"

The three girls exited the bus and into the public.

"So, what do you think?" Max asked El excitedly.

El frowned.

"Hey, what's wrong?" Max asked her.

"Too many people against the rules." El replied.

"Seriously? Tara goes here all the time!" Max exclaimed.

"Joyce doesn't stop her from leaving." El said.

"El, you have superpowers! What's the worst that could happen?" Max asked with a reassuring grin.

They went into the mall and El looked around in awe.

"So, what should we do first?" Max asked before her eyes widened. "You've never been shopping before, have you?"

El shook her head no.

"Well then, I guess we're gonna have to try on everything." Max said before her eyes sparkled to life.

"Ooh! Come on!" Max spoke as she led them over to a clothing store.

Max grinned as El looked through many shirts.

El's eyes laid upon a piece of clothing that caught her eye.

"Do you like that?" Max asked her.

"How do I know what I like?" El asked.

"You just try things on. Until you find something that feels like you." Max replied.

"Like me?" El questioned.

Max smiled softly.

"Yeah. Not Hopper. Not Mike. You." Max replied.

El smiled to herself.

El tried on a couple dresses in front of the mirror.

Max spun her around as El giggled.

She didn't even worry about Mike right now.

Max tried on a few sunglasses while Tara found a sweater she liked. It was

Max had tried to tell her it was summer but Tara insisted.

El fluffed up her hair as Max grinned.

El practically dragged Max and Tara out of the store with a wide smile.

They linked arms as they skipped along together.

Next, Max took them over to a photo shooting place.

They put on fancy clothing, the kind you'd see in magazines.

"That's it, girls! Here we go!" A man chirped as he took photographs of them.

They struck a couple poses, feeling at their best.

"Shake it out for me." The man demonstrated.

The trio shook out their hair, grinning.

Next up, they tried on high heels.

Max helped the two walk, but Tara collapsed onto El, who accidentally brought Max to the floor.

They fell into a fit of giggles despite seeing a group of girls who glared at them in annoyance.

That just made them laugh harder.

Max helped the two stand up before El got an idea.

El focused on the girls' drinks and with her mind, she made the drink burst.

Max let out a giggle of awe as the three bolted off.

"See? What'd I tell you?" Max said to El. "There's more to life than--"

"Stupid boys!" El replied, giggling.

"How about we get ice cream next?" Max asked.

Tara's eyes lit up.

"Yes." Tara responded.

They made a quick stop at Scoops Ahoy.

"Okay, here you go, you got a strawberry, one chocolate and then a vanilla with sprinkles, extra whipped cream." Steve said as he handed the girls their ice creams.

"Thanks." They responded in unison and began licking their ice creams.

Steve frowned as he looked at El.

"Wait a second. Are you even allowed to be here?" He asked.

El glanced at Max and Tara before giggling.

They ran off, leaving a very confused Steve.

"That-- Okay." He muttered.

Max, El, and Tara exited the mall as happy as ever.

Max frowned in annoyance.

"You've gotta be shitting me." She cursed.

El and Tara turned their heads to where she was looking and saw Mike, Lucas and Will.

They approached the boys.

"Isn't this a nice surprise?" Max asked with a smirk. She loved to piss Mike off.

Mike dropped his bike dramatically.

"What are you doing here?" He asked El.

"Shopping." El replied coldly, glaring at him.

"This is her new style; what do you think?" Max asked Mike sarcastically.

"What's wrong with you? You know she's not allowed to be here." Mike told her with frustration.

"What is she, your little pet?" Max asked.

"Yeah, am I your pet?" El asked angrily.

"What? No!" Mike replied quickly.

"Then why do you treat me like Garbage?" El asked.

"What?" Mike asked. He was genuinely confused.

"Don't lie. Friend's don't lie." Tara told him.

"I'm not lying!" Mike exclaimed.

"You said Nana was sick." El reminded him.

Mike's eyes widened.

"She is sick!" Mike said while nudging Lucas.

"She's super sick. That's why we're here actually." Lucas lied.

"Yeah, we're shopping. Not for us but for her. For Nana." Mike said.

"For Nana!" Lucas added, seeming a little too enthusiastic for a lie.

"Also, we're here to get a gift for you. But we couldn't find anything that suited you and I only have $3.50 so it's hard." Mike lied.

"Super hard. It's expensive." Lucas added.

"You lie." El snapped at him. "Why do you lie?"

Mike's mouth dropped open as he searched his brain to find an excuse.

El huffed with anger.

She walked closer to him.

"I dump your ass." She told him.

Max and Tara's jaw dropped open in shock.

The three girls skipped onto the bus and high-fived one another.

THIRTEEN

"You must be an angel. I can see it in your eyes." Max sang as she held El's hairbrush like a microphone.

El opened up one of Max's magazines.

On the cover was Ralph Maccio.

"Oh you found Ralph Maccio!" Max chuckled.

"Maccio?" El asked with amusement.

"Yeah! He's the karate kid!" Max replied as she demonstrated karate.

Tara let out a soft giggle.

"He's so hot, right?" Max asked.

"Hot?" Tara asked.

"Yeah it's like, when somebody's so good looking. So-" Max explained.

"Pretty. So pretty." Tara said as she cut her off.

"Like Ralph. I bet he's an amazing kisser too." Max said.

El shot her a weird look.

"Hey uh, is Mike a good kisser?" Max asked.

"I don't know; he's my first boyfriend." El replied.

"Ex boyfriend." Max corrected.

El's smile faltered.

Max readjusted her seat.

"Hey don't worry about it, okay? He'll come crawling back to you in no time, begging for forgiveness. I guarantee you, he's totally wallowing in self pity right now. He's like, Oh I hope she takes me back!" Max dramatically said to El.

The three of them giggled.

"God, what I wouldn't give to see their stupid faces!" Max exclaimed.

El bit her bottom lip; she definitely had an idea.

They set up the radio as El wrapped a blindfold over her eyes.

El sat down cross legged on her bedroom floor.

"Is this really going to work?" Max asked with excitement.

El and Tara nodded.

"Holy shit, this is insane!" Max exclaimed.

"Max." El said firmly.

Tara put her finger on Max's lips.

"Quiet. I'm sorry." Max said to herself.

"I see them." El said after a few moments.

"What are they doing?" Max asked curiously.

"Eating." El replied. "They say we are species."

Max's eyes widened.

"What?" She asked.

"Emotion not logic." El added.

Max went bewildered.

El suddenly ripped the blindfold off and her eyes went wide with fear or shock.

"El?" Tara asked worriedly.

A small smile came from El's lips as she fell down laughing.

"Wh-What?" Max asked, giggling along with her.

The girls suddenly sat up straight as they heard the sound of a familiar car.

Hopper's.

El quickly wiped her nose as Max reached for three magazines.

"Copy me." Max whispered as she laid down on the bedroom floor and picked up the magazine.

She started looking at it as if that's what she'd been doing this entire time.

El and Tara did the same just as Hopper slammed the front door open.

El switched on her radio and played some pop music.

"Hey!" Hopper growled as he stormed over to El's bedroom door.

"When I say three inches, three-" Hopper said as he threw open her bedroom door.

Instead of Mike, he saw El was with Max and Tara.

"Do you knock? Jeez!" Max exclaimed as Hopper's jaw dropped in disbelief.

"Yeah, jeez." El added.

Tara shook her head at him, acting disappointed with his actions.

"I'm sorry!" Hopper quickly apologized. "I thought that--"

"Mike's not here." Max said.

"Max and Tara wanted to have a sleepover." El told him. "Is that okay?"

"Yeah. Yeah. Yeah. Your parents know about it?" Hopper asked the two.

"Yup." Max confirmed.

"Joyce'll be okay with it." Tara said.

"Yeah, it's cool. Really cool." Hopper said, slurring his words drunkenly.

He stared at them and they stared back in confusion.

"Did you need something?" Max asked.

"No, I'll leave." Hopper said as he closed the bedroom door gently.

"Holy shit. I can't believe we're doing this." Max commented as she wrote down a few names.

"Ready?" Max said.

"Ready." El and Tara said in unison.

They were playing spin the bottle. Not the kind you'd think though!

Tara gripped the bottle firmly as she spun it.

The bottle landed on Mr. Wheeler.

Max frowned in disgust.

"Ugh boring." She commented.

"Yeah boring." El repeated with a smile.

"Spin again." Max told Tara.

Tara went to spin the bottle but El gently grasped her wrist.

"That's against the rules." El spoke.

"We make our own rules." Max said.

El chuckled as she released Tara's wrist.

Tara spun the bottle and it landed on Billy.

"Billy." The three said in unison.

Tara frowned before nervously giggling.

Max stood up before fetching the radio.

"Okay look, I should just warn you, if he's with a girl or doing something gross, get out of there before your scarred for life." Max told her out of concern.

"Max--" Tara began.

"No I'm just saying. He's really gross!" Max exclaimed.

"Max, let her spy." El told her.

"Okay shutting up now." Max said before tuning the radio.

Max put the blindfold over Tara's eyes.

Tara took a deep breath and focused on Billy.

The first thing Tara saw was a car.

"I see a car. Billy's." Tara reported to El and Max.

Tara peered her head inside the car but didn't find Billy.

But then she heard a quiet whimper.

She saw Billy kneeling on the ground.

"I found Billy." Tara said.

"What's he doing?" Max asked.

"I don't know- He's on the floor." Tara explained what she was seeing. She realized what she was saying seemed like he wasn't okay. "He's okay. He's talking to someone."

Tara approached Billy.

The whimpering sounds got louder and more fearful.

Billy stood up and he abruptly turned around.

He looked at Tara straight in the eyes.

Tara's eyes widened. He shouldn't be able to see her.

Then, she heard a scream. A scream of terror and pain.

Tara had enough and ripped her blindfold off.

"What happened?" El asked.

"I don't know..." Tara whispered.

The three girls walked over to Max's house as clouds approached them above.

"It's gonna start pouring soon. We should be at the mall or watching a movie." Max said.

"You don't believe her?" El asked Max, referring to Tara.

"Believe Tara? Of course I do." Max quickly said. "It's just, El, you said Mike has sensed you in there before right? So maybe it was just like that. Maybe Billy sensed Tara somehow."

"But I've never met him." Tara said as she frowned with confusion.

"But Tara said there were screams." El said.

"Yeah I know but here's the thing. When Billy is alone with a girl, they make really crazy noises." Max said.

"They scream?" El asked with uncertainty.

"Yeah but like, happy screams." Max said.

"Happy screams?" Tara asked as she frowned in confusion.

"Yeah um, I'll tell you later." Max said with a knowing grin.

"What?" Tara asked.

"Just don't tell Mike." Max added with a dramatic gulp.

El's face went serious as she stared at Max's house.

"You really wanna do this?" Max asked the two girls.

They both nodded.

Max gently pushed open Billy's bedroom door.

Tara glanced around; noticing many pictures of exposed girls on his wall and more.

Max walked over to a drawer and pulled it open.

She found an inappropriate magazine.

She frowned in disgust.

"Ugh, gag me with a spoon!" She exclaimed as she quickly pushed the drawer shut.

Next, they went into the bathroom.

They didn't find anything suspicious, until they looked at the bathtub.

They found packs of ice lying in a bath filled with water already.

"It's just ice." Max reassured the two girls. "Probably for his muscles or something. He works out like a maniac."

Out of the corner of her eye, Tara noticed blood on a cabinet.

Her breathing hitched as she pulled the cabinet open.

Inside, was a yellow whistle.

It was covered in blood.

They stopped off at the swimming center and walked up to two people who worked there.

"Excuse me." Max said.

"No one in the water until 30 minutes after the last strike. And don't try and argue with me. If you want to get electrocuted, go climb a tree." The man replied back, his eyes on his newspaper.

"Yeah we don't care. We're not here to swim." Max replied back. "Or get electrocuted."

El pulled out a bag that belonged to one of the people who worked there.

The man finally looked up at the three girls.

"Does that belong to anybody here?" Max asked.

"Oh yeah, that's Heather's. I'll get it back to her." The man replied.

"We could give it back to her." El quickly said.

"You could. Except she's not here." He said. "Bailed on me today."

They all shot each other a look.

"What is this? You girls want a reward or something?" He asked them.

"No, we're just good Samaritans." Max said with a pretend smile.

"Heather." Max said as they walked up to a picture of Heather, a life guard. "Do you think you guys can find her?"

"I will." Tara said.

Tara pulled the picture of Heather off the wall.

The dynamic trio made their way into the restroom.

Max turned on all the showers as El handed Tara somebody's swimming goggles.

Tara put the swimming goggles on and closed her eyes.

The first thing she saw was a mailbox.

It read '1438'.

Then, a red door appeared.

"What do you see?" Max asked.

"What is it?" El asked as well.

"A red door." Tara responded.

Tara pushed open the door and found a bathtub.

A part of her felt tense, and she didn't know why.

She cautiously walked up to the bathtub.

The bathtub was filled with ice, much like the one in Billy's bathroom.

A girl shot out of the bathtub with wide eyes.

"Help me!" She pleaded before she was dragged back under the water.

Tara's eyes enlarged as she fell down onto the water beneath her feet.

Tara threw the swimming goggles off and her breathing was heavy.

"What happened?" Max asked as she quickly wrapped her arms around Tara.

"Tara..." El said in worry. She didn't like not knowing what was going on.

They biked over to where Tara said the red door was.

It was also pouring with rain but that didn't stop them.

"Is this it?" Max asked.

Tara nodded.

They went up to the door and El threw the door open with her mind.

The first thing they saw when they walked in, was a photo.

On the photo had three people.

Two unfamiliar adults and Heather.

"This is Heather's house." Max realized.

They heard laughing so they walked over to where the laughing had come from.

Much to their surprise, they found a man, a woman and... Billy.

"Max." Billy said with surprise.

"We didn't mean to barge in. We tried to knock but maybe you didn't hear us over the storm." Max lied.

"I'm sorry, who is this dripping all over my living room right now?" The man asked unimpressed.

"I'm sorry." Billy said with a chuckle as he went over to the girls.

"Janet, Tom, this is my sister Maxine!" Billy chirped enthusiastically.

Tara heard bad things about Billy from Max. But strangely enough, he sounded way too happy to see Max.

"What on earth are you doing here?" He asked Max, his voice high pitch. "Is something wrong?"

"We just wanted to make sure everything was okay." Max said.

"Okay? Why wouldn't it be okay?" Billy asked.

Tara cleared her throat to get his attention.

"Where is she?" She asked, glaring at him.

"I'm sorry, where is who?" He asked.

"Well, they're a little burnt, I'm sorry--" Heather said as she walked into the room.

"Heather! This is my sister Maxine, and I'm sorry I did not quite catch your guys's names." Billy said, turning to El and Tara."

"El."

"Tara." Tara replied, staring at him right in the eyes.

"El. Tara." Billy spoke with a hint of realization.

Tara felt there was something oddly familiar about him. But she couldn't quite figure out what.

"Now, what is it you were saying, Tara?" Billy asked. "You were looking for somebody?"

"S-She saw..." El stuttered.

"Your manager. At the pool. He said you guys didn't come in to work today, so we got worried." Max quickly spoke over El.

"Heather wasn't feeling so hot today. So we thought we'd take the day off to nurse her back to health." Billy said before looking at Heather expectantly. "But you're feeling just fine right now, aren't you Heather?"

"I'm feeling so much better." Heather confirmed.

Tara felt herself unable to look away from Billy's eyes. She felt like she knew his eyes from somewhere.

"Do you girls want a cookie?" Heather asked kindly.

The three girls left the house and hopped onto their bikes; as Billy watched. His eye pupils dilating dangerously.

FOURTEEN

That night, El got into bed with Tara and Max.

"Which one? Tara can't decide." Max asked El with a smile.

"I don't know." El said.

"Hey, there's nothing to worry about anymore, okay?" Max said to reassure her.

"It doesn't make sense." El said.

"What doesn't make sense?" Max asked.

"Heather. The blood, the ice," El listed.

"Heather had a fever so she took a cold bath but she's better now." Max said. "That has to be it. I don't know where that blood came from but we all saw her. She's totally fine."

"What about Billy?" El asked. "He seemed wrong."

Max opened her mouth to talk but Tara cut her off.

"El isn't wrong. He looked at me like," Tara paused as she recalled what happened. "Like he knew me. I felt like I knew him. Something so famili ar."

"It's probably just me rambling about how shitty he is." Max joked.

El suddenly frowned.

"Who is that?" She asked, pointing at one of Max's magazines.

"See, this is why you can't just hang out with Mike all the time. This is Wonder woman. AKA Princess Diana. She's from Paradise Island which is like this hidden island where there are only women amazon warriors." Max explained.

It was really early in the morning, when Tara heard a voice from her walkie.

She didn't answer immediately, and looked at the time.

The sun was barley up.

Tara answered the walkie while being half asleep. "Yes?"

"Good, you're awake. Meet me at Scoops." Dustin said quickly.

"But--" Tara began.

"No time to explain!" Dustin cut her off. "Over and out."

He turned the walkie off.

Tara glanced at El and Max and saw they were still asleep.

She wrote down on a piece of paper.

Dustin needs me. Be right back.

Tara-

Tara made her way to where Steve worked and pushed the door open to where Steve and Robin would sometimes hang out.

"What took you so long?" Dustin complained.

"No bike." Tara replied.

Dustin made a small 'o' shape with his mouth.

Steve furrowed his eyebrows at Tara.

"She should know." Dustin shrugged innocently.

"Know what?" Tara asked.

"Well--" Dustin was cut off when the door opened once more.

"It is fascinating what 20 bucks will get you at the county records office." Robin said as she led out a map or something.

"Starcourt Mall." She revealed proudly. "The complete blueprints."

"Not bad." Dustin complimented.

"So this is us, Scoops, and this is where we want to get," Robin explained with her finger.

"I mean, I don't really see a way in." Steve muttered.

"There's not. If you're talking exclusively about doors." Robin replied.

"Air ducts." Dustin realized.

"Exactly." Robin grinned at him. "Turns out this secret room needs air just like any old room. And these air ducts lead all the way here."

Steve took off the lid to a vent.

"Flashlight." Steve asked.

Dustin handed Steve the flashlight.

Steve flicked on the flashlight and peered his head inside the vent.

"Yeah I don't know if you can fit, it's super tight." Steve told Dustin.

"I can fit." Dustin assured him. "Trust me. No collar bones, remember?"

"Excuse me?" Robin asked with surprise.

"Oh he's got some disease. It's chrydo, something." Steve explained.

"It's badass." Tara complimented.

"He's missing bones and stuff. He can bend like Gumbo." Steve added.

"Pretty sure it's Gumby." Robin corrected.

"Steve, just shut up and push me!" Dustin yelled.

"Okay!" Steve shouted back as he grabbed Dustin's feet and began to push.

"Not my feet dumbass. Push my ass." Dustin told him.

"What?" Steve asked.

"Touch my butt! I don't care!" Dustin yelled out of frustration.

Steve placed his hands on Dustin's behind and began pushing.

Robin shook her head at them.

A bell rung from behind them.

"Ahoy Sailors! All hands on deck!" Erica spoke impatiently.

Robin's eyes sparkled to life with a brilliant idea.

Erica peered up into the vent and hummed to herself.

"Yeah, I don't know." She said to the others.

"You don't know if you can fit?" Dustin asked.

"Oh, I can fit. I just don't know if I want to." Erica replied.

"Are you Claustrophobic?" Robin asked.

"I don't have phobias." Erica replied with a snort of amusement.

"What's the problem?" Steve asked impatiently.

"The problem is, I still haven't heard what's in this, for Erica." Erica explained.

"You see this? This is the route you're gonna take. Then we just wait until the last delivery goes out tonight. Then you knock out the grate, jump down, open the door." Robin explained.

"Exactly." Robin confirmed.

"And you say this guard is armed." Erica recalled.

"Yes but he won't be there." Dustin assured her.

"And booby traps?" Erica asked. "Lasers, spikes in the wall..."

Robin grinned with amusement.

"You know what this half baked plan of yours sounds like to me? Child endangerment." Erica snapped at them.

"We'll be in radio contact with you the whole time--" Robin began.

"Child endangerment!" Erica cut her off.

"Erica?" Dustin called out as Erica turned to him. "We think these russians want to do harm to our country. Great harm. Don't you love your country?"

"You can't spell America without Erica." Erica said.

"Oddly, that's totally true." Dustin realized. "So, don't do this for us. Do this for America. Erica."

"Ooh! I just got the chills!" Erica exclaimed.

Dustin grinned.

"Oh yeah, from this float. Not your speech." She added.

Dustin's smile dropped.

"Know what I love most about this country?" Erica asked. "Capitalism. You know what Capitalism is?"

"Yeah." Dustin and Robin said.

"No." Tara said.

"It means this is a free market system which means people get paid for their services, depending on how valuable their contributions are. And it seems to me, my ability to fit into that little vent is very valuable to you. So you want my help?" Erica said.

"We do anything." Tara quickly said, knowing how desperate Dustin and Steve were. No one had still filled her in.

"Anything? Then I want free ice cream. For life." Erica demanded.

It took some time but Erica finally made it into the vent and into that room.

The others ran into the room she was in.

They found the boxes.

Steve opened one of the boxes and opened some sort of jar.

Inside, was some type of green goo.

"What the hell?" Steve quietly muttered to himself.

The room suddenly shook.

"Is that just me or did the room move?" Dustin asked nervously.

"You know what? Let's just grab that and go." Robin said as she grabbed the jar.

Dustin pressed the button to open the door.

"Which one do I press Erica?" He asked.

"Just press the damn button, nerd." Erica snapped.

Tara sighed as she moved her head to open the door with her mind but a wall closed over the door.

The room jerked, and they were thrown to the floor.

The room was in fact an elevator and the elevator was going down, at a very fast speed.

"Oh shit." Steve cursed aloud.

FIFTEEN

They all screamed as they were thrown back and fourth across the elevator.

"We're going down!" Steve yelled out of panic.

"Yeah no shit, Harrington!" Robin yelled back.

"Why don't these buttons work?" Dustin shouted.

Then, the elevator jerking suddenly stopped.

They fell down once more.

Tara winced and was dazed.

A large box fell onto Steve.

"My groin. It fell on my groin." Steve complained as he struggled underneath it.

Dustin lifted the box off Steve.

Tara slowly stood up to her feet, her head slightly spinning.

"Is everyone okay?" Robin asked.

Tara stumbled a bit, regaining her breath.

"Yeah I'm great now that I know russians can't design elevators!" Steve yelled at Robin.

"Woah, you're alright?" Dustin asked Tara who nodded.

"I think we've clearly established those buttons don't do anything." Robin said to Steve, who was still frantically pressing buttons.

"They're buttons! They have to do something!" Steve snapped at her.

"Yeah, if we had a keycard." Robin said. "It's an electronic lock. Same as the loading dock door. If we don't have a keycard, it won't operate meaning--"

"We're stuck in here." Dustin realized.

"Just so you nerds are aware, I'm supposed to be spending the night at Tina's, and Tina always covers for me. But if I'm not home for Uncle Jack's party tomorrow and my mom finds out that you four are responsible, she's gonna hunt you down one by one, and slit your throats!" Erica threatens.

Tara was seriously losing her patience with her.

"I don't care about Tina, or Uncle Jack's party! Your mom's not going to be able to find us if we're dead in a Russian elevator!" Steve snapped at her.

"Won't die." Tara assured him. "Promise."

"You talk funny." Erica mutters sarcastically.

Dustin suddenly pointed upwards.

"Hey. What if we climbed out?" Dustin asked.

They got up onto the second floor and the ceiling was very tall.

As someone had been in the elevator, they left so Scoops Troop quickly jumped down and Steve placed the mysterious jar down to keep the door from closing.

They quickly slid under the door just before the jar shattered.

"Oh, jesus." Dustin whined.

They turned around, only to find an incredibly long corridor.

"Hope you guys are in good shape. Looking at you, Roast Beef." Steve said to Dustin as he began to walk.

The others followed him.

"I mean, you have to admit; as a feat of engineering alone, this is impress ive." Dustin said in awe.

"What are you talking about? It's a total fire hazard. There's no stairs, there's no exit. There's just an elevator that drops you halfway to hell." Steve said.

"They're commies. You don't pay people; they cut corners." Erica told him.

"To be fair to our russian commies, I don't think this tunnel was designed for walking." Robin said. "Think about it; they developed the perfect system for transporting that cargo."

"It all comes into the mall like any old delivery." Dustin said.

"And then they load it up onto those trucks and nobody's the wiser." Robin added.

"You think they built this whole mall so they could transport that green poison?" Steve asked.

"I very seriously doubt it's something as boring as poison." Steve murmured.

"It's probably being used to make something." Dustin said.

"Or transport something." Robin said.

"Like a nuclear weapon." Dustin said.

"Exactly." Robin agreed.

"Walking towards a nuclear weapon. That's great." Steve said sarcastically.

"But if they're building something, why here?" Robin asked. "I mean, Hawkins. Of all places!"

Tara suddenly stopped as she realized.

Steve and Dustin walked to her side.

"You think the Russians know?" Dustin asked.

"About--" Steve began.

"Maybe." Tara whispered.

"So it's connected?" Steve whispered back.

"How?" Dustin whispered.

"And why?" Tara whispered.

"I don't know but it's..." Steve trailed off.

"Possible." Tara, Steve and Dustin whispered in unison.

"I'm sorry, is there something you'd like to share with the class?" Robin asked them.

The walkie suddenly went off.

They rushed over to the walkie.

"A trip to china sounds nice. If you tread lightly." Robin said in Russian.

"It's the code." Robin added in English.

"Wherever that broadcast is coming from--" Dustin began.

"It's close." Robin said. "And if there's one thing that we know about that signal..."

"It can reach the surface." Dustin said.

"Let's go." Robin said with a grin.

They made it out of the tunnel and out into the open, surrounded by Russians.

Nobody noticed them.

They silently snuck into a room.

Their eyes enlarged as they realized they weren't alone.

A russian stared at them in bewilderment.

Tara tilted her head to the side, and the man's neck snapped.

He fell lifeless to the floor.

She could her her own heart pounding as blood dripped from her nose.

"Holy shit! What happened? How did--" Robin stumbled over her words in shock.

"Tara has superpowers." Dustin said casually.

Tara nodded to confirm.

"She doesn't look well." Erica said. She probably could've said that in a better way.

"Whenever she uses her powers, she gets drained." Dustin explained as he slung his arm around her to help balance her.

"You didn't have to kill him!" Steve exclaimed.

While they weren't looking, Robin walked up the steps and glanced through a window.

She saw a bright blue light.

"Guys!" She called. "There's something up here."

They followed after her and looked through the window.

"Holy shit." Dustin cursed.

"Oh no." Tara whispered as she recognized the sight in front of her.

The Gate.

SIXTEEN

"The Gate." Steve, Dustin and Tara whispered together.

"I don't understand; you've seen this before?" Robin asked.

"Not exactly." Steve murmured.

"All you need to know is it's bad." Dustin quickly said.

"It's really bad." Steve added.

"Like, the end of the human race as we know it kind of bad." Dustin rambled.

"And you know about this how?" Robin asked in disbelief.

The alarm suddenly went off.

Dustin grabbed Tara's hand and they all dashed away like a bat out of hell.

Tara was struggling.

Whenever she got drained, much like El, she'd need rest. She wasn't getting rest.

They ran into a room and quickly slammed the door behind them.

Steve and Robin pressed their backs against the door, protecting Dustin, Erica and Tara.

"Go! Just get out of here!" Steve yelled to them. "Get some help!"

"Wait. I-I can teleport to the others. I can get help." Tara suggested.

"Telepo- She can teleport?" Robin asked whilst struggling as the Russians rammed their bodies against the door.

"How is that even important right now?!" Steve yelled to her. "Just- Guys, go!"

Tara closed her eyes and thought of El's cabin.

That's where Max and El were last.

"...they've obviously vanished off the face of the Earth. So can we please come up with a new plan because I love her and I can't lose her again?!"

Tara heard Mike shout.

She opened her eyes and found herself with the others.

She fell backwards and Max caught her.

El went over with confusion and relief.

"What's going on? When'd you-" She asked.

"Nothing, nothing!" Mike quickly said.

"Just having a family discussion." Lucas joked.

"Oh." El said before looking expectantly at Tara.

Tara sat herself down on the couch; out of breath.

"I was at the mall." Tara explained. "Then they- bad. Gate. I-I... They've got Steve and Robin."

Nancy frowned in utter confusion.

"I found him." El said, to clear the silence.

"Found who?" Nancy asked.

"And that's not normal, right?" Nancy asked Max.

"Billy staying in his room on the fourth of July? No, that's not normal." Max replied.

"He wants us to find him." Will said.

"Yeah, that's what I'm afraid of. If we go to Billy, then the rest of the Flayed know where we are." Nancy said.

"It's a trap; I agree. We'll be ambushed." Mike added.

"We won't be surprised. We'll know that they're coming and we will kick their flayed butts." Lucas said.

"You mean El and Tara will kick their butts." Max corrected him.

"It's too risky." Mike said.

"Yeah and unnecessary." Nancy said. "Killing the Flayed won't stop the Mind Flayer. We have to find out where it's spreading from. We have to find the source."

El walked into the room.

"Billy knows. He's been there." She told the others. "It's a trap, I know. We can't go to Billy but I think there's another way for me to see where he's been."

"I can." Tara said.

"Tar, you're too weak." Mike reminded her.

"Mike, relax." Max said as she rolled her eyes at him.

"Well, I'm sorry for caring!" He snapped at her. "Just-"

"I can do it myself." El said confidently.

"El, I know you think you have to do this but you don't. It's just, you've only done this before once. And your mom, she loved you and wanted you to know what happened," Mike told El as Max scoffed.

"And Billy's mind is sick- diseased. The Mind Flayer is in him." Mike added in worry.

"He can't hurt me. Not in there." El told him.

"We don't know that." Mike replied.

El took Mike's hand in hers and gazed up at him.

"Mike, I need you to trust me." She asked.

Mike glanced at Max who gave him a look.

Mike hesitantly nodded at El.

El placed the blindfold over her eyes.

"I'm on a beach." El reported back to the others.

"I may be dense but the last time I checked, there were no beaches in Hawkins." Lucas joked.

"What else do you see?" Max asked curiously.

"A woman. She's pretty." El replied. "I-I think she's looking at me."

"There's a boy." She added. "It's Billy."

"It's California. A memory." Max realized.

A few moments, El said. "I see it. The source."

"Where are you, El?" Max asked.

"Brimborns Steelworks." El responded.

It was silence before El screamed out as she threw her blindfold off.

She hyperventilated with anxiety, as Mike wrapped his arms around her.

SEVENTEEN

"He said he was building something. All for me and Tara." El told the others what she saw. What Billy was telling her.

"Building something, is he talking about the Flayed?" Max questioned.

"Must be." Nancy said.

"So he's building an army, like we thought." Lucas said.

"Yeah but he's not building this army to spread." Mike said.

"He's building it to stop Eleven and Twelve." Will said.

"Last year, El and Tara closed the gate on him. I have a feeling that pissed him off." Mike said.

"Like, royally." Lucas added.

"And the Mind Flayer now knows that they are the only things that can stop him. But if they're out of the way--" Mike said.

"Game over." Lucas said.

"He also said he was going to kill all of you." El said.

"Ah well, that's nice." Max sarcastically said.

"Do you guys hear that?" Nancy asked.

"It's just the fireworks." Jonathan reassured her.

"El, when Billy told you all that, it was here, in this room?" Nancy asked El.

El nodded.

Nancy's eyes enlarged.

Will slowly raised his hand up to his neck.

"He knows we're here."

They rushed out of the house, and they saw a moving figure in the trees.

The Mind Flayer was coming.

They rushed back into the house as the older teens grabbed weapons.

They boarded up the windows.

They stood next to one another, waiting for its attack.

But it was just pure silence.

Then, a tentacle broke through the wall and went straight for El.

El backed away, in front of Max and Will.

Jonathan slashed it with an axe.

The tentacle snarled and tossed Jonathan aside. He hit the wall hard.

The tentacle crept closer to Jonathan, but Tara held it back angrily.

She'd grown close to Jonathan, and there was no way she'd let it hurt him.

"No." She said as she dragged it above her head.

El took over and screamed; snapping the tentacle in half.

It slid back out of the wall.

"Are you okay?" Tara asked Max, who was by the tentacle.

"Yeah--"

Max got cut off when the tentacle lunged itself at El but Tara held it back with her mind.

The other tentacle came and El held that one back.

Tara threw the two tentacles and they snapped.

There was this disgusting goo all over El's cabin floor now.

What they didn't expect was, The Mind Flayer broke a hole through the ceiling.

It grabbed onto El's leg. It dragged her upwards, but Mike quickly grabbed her arm.

Tara threw out her arm but a tentacle grabbed her arm.

Tara screamed as Mike's other hand went to Tara's leg.

They all grabbed onto Tara and El, desperately pulling.

The harder they pulled, the tighter the Mind Flayer's tentacles gripped onto El's leg and Tara's arm.

Nancy shot at the Mind Flayer.

"Come on! Lucas!" Max yelled.

Lucas grabbed an axe and very swiftly slashed at the tentacles with it.

"Pull!" Max yelled, desperate to save her girlfriend and best friend.

With Lucas slashing with the axe and Nancy shooting, the tentacle gave up and El and Tara fell.

"Oh god, I thought I was going to loose you," Max said worriedly as she helped Tara up. "You're okay?"

It was then Max's eyes trailed over to Tara's arm.

Her arm was severely hurt. It was bleeding badly.

"That- I-," Max stammered as her eyes went wide with concern.

El stumbled to her feet, wheezing in pain.

Tara threw her arms out, despite the great pain in her arm.

Together, El and Tara attacked the Mind Flayer.

It screeched in pain.

"Go!" Nancy yelled as Max helped El walk.

Mike wrapped his arm over El, to also help her walk.

They rushed into the car and helped El inside.

El rested her head on Mike's shoulder, whimpering in pain.

"Drive!" Mike yelled to Nancy.

Nancy took off driving.

Nancy pulled up at a store.

Tara saw a rock and threw it at the wall with her mind.

"Badass?" Tara whispered to Max.

"Very." Max replied.

They entered the closed store, and laid El down on the store floor.

Tara sat down.

"Stay still; both of you." Nancy told Tara and El as she prepared to clean their wounds.

"Woah," Max said, placing an arm on Nancy's to stop her. "What are you doing?"

"I'm cleaning the wounds." Nancy said.

"No, first we need to stop the bleeding, then clean, then disinfect, then bandage." Max said casually.

Everyone shot her a look.

"I skateboard, trust me." She quickly added.

Max placed a piece of paper down onto El's leg and one onto Tara's.

"Mike, do you mind?" Max asked.

Mike placed his hands onto El's leg and Tara's arm, putting pressure on the wounds.

Tara hissed in pain.

"We're gonna need water, soap," Max said before looking expectantly at Nancy and Jonathan.

They quickly rose to their feet and left on search for water and soap.

Lucas brought out his backpack and emptied it.

Max frowned with confusion.

"Does any of this help?" He asked innocently.

"No." Max replied, annoyed. "Go get me a washcloth and a bowl."

"A bowl?" Lucas asked.

"Lucas." Max growled.

Will nudged him. "Go." He whispered.

"Okay!" Lucas quickly said before leaving with Will.

Max growled again, "Why are they taking so long? All I asked was a bowl and washcloth."

Max rushed over to them, leaving Tara with Mike and El.

Mike was in the middle of talking to El when a voice on his walkie spoke.

A voice she'd recognize anywhere.

"I repeat, this is a code red!" Dustin said, his voice almost incoherent.

Mike scrambled to his feet and answered the walkie.

"Dustin?" Mike asked.

"Mike!" Dustin exclaimed. "Oh my god, you have to listen. I know tha- MIA. I've been mad. Trapped secre- base."

"Dustin, I can't understand you." Mike told him.

"I know, insane, rus, infia- Kins!" Dustin said, his voice breaking up now.

Tara strained her hearing to try to understand him better.

"Now, they're using to open the gate!" That was the only thing they could make out of what Dustin was saying.

"Dustin, you're breaking up!" Mike told him.

Once Tara's leg was bandaged, she inhaled deeply.

"I can go to them. El won't have to spy." Tara told them.

"Yeah, do it." Mike said.

"Now, who's the one using girlfriends?" Max muttered.

Tara closed her eyes and disappeared from plain sight.

She reappeared somewhere in Starcourt mall. In a bathroom.

"You'll be holding on forever!" Robin and Steve sang together before breaking into a fit of giggling.

Tara cleared her throat.

Robin and Steve let out a scream.

To make it even more awkward, Dustin threw the restroom door open, Erica by his side.

"What the he- Tara! Where've you bee- Your arm!" Dustin exclaimed.

"It's badass." Tara said.

They went out into the main area of Starcourt mall.

"We just have to get on the bus with the rest of these plebes, and home sweet home, here we come." Dustin said with a proud grin.

Steve's face went pale.

"Uh, Dustin?" Steve murmured nervously.

"What?" Dustin asked.

"We might not want to go to your house." Steve said.

"Why?" Dustin asked.

"Well, I might've told them your full name." Steve explained.

"What is wrong with you?" Dustin hissed.

"Dude, I was drugged!" Steve said.

"So! You resist. You tough it out like a man!" Dustin snapped at him.

"Oh yeah, it's easy for you to say." Steve sarcastically said.

"Guys?" Robin nervously spoke.

Robin grabbed Tara's shoulder, gently pulling her back.

There was a man.

"Abort." Dustin whispered.

They took off running.

They all slid down the wall of an escalator.

Dustin grabbed Tara and pulled her down. They all hid down behind a stall.

Their breathing hitched as the men drew closer.

Tara teleported behind them.

"Hi." She said as she threw a couple of them aside. Then, she snapped their necks.

A loud crunch echoed across the mall as they dropped lifeless and dead to the floor.

The man in front of her turned bewildered; gun pointed at her.

A sudden car alarm rang.

Tara and the man turned around in shock.

They raised their heads to find El, Max, Mike, Lucas, Nancy and Jonathan.

Tara quickly teleported next to them.

This was for sure as hell draining her power.

El had her hand extended, before throwing the car at the man.

The car rammed him into the wall. He was no longer a problem.

Tara stumbled into Max.

"Hey, I got you. You're fine," Max said as she wrapped an arm around Tara. "I got you. You're okay?"

Tara gave a slight head nod.

El smiled as they all ran up to Dustin, Erica, Robin and Steve.

"You flung that thing like a hot wheel! And you Tara, you are my savior." Dustin grinned.

Lucas frowned at seeing his younger sister.

"Lucas!" Erica called.

"What are you doing here?" He asked in disbelief.

"Ask them. It's their fault." Erica said, pointing to Steve and Robin.

"Totally true. It's absolutely our fault." Steve agreed.

"Child endangerment." Tara added innocently.

Dustin mentally face palmed.

"I don't understand what happened to that car. So what, who else has powers?!" Robin exclaimed, dazed from it all.

"El also has superpowers." Dustin replied.

"Yeah, she threw it with her mind. Like how Tara snapped their necks. C'mon, catch up." Steve said to Robin.

"That's El?" Erica asked with amazement.

"Who's El?" Robin asked.

"I'm sorry, who are you?" Nancy asked.

"I'm Robin; I work with Steve." Robin said.

"She's badass." Tara complimented with a small smile.

Robin grinned back.

"And she cracked the top secret code." Dustin added.

"Yeah, which is how we found out about the russians in the first place." Steve said.

"What russians?" Jonathan asked.

"The russians!" Steve exclaimed, frustrated.

"Those were russians?" Max asked in shock.

"Yes." Tara replied casually.

"What do you mean?" Lucas asked.

"Didn't you hear our code red?" Dustin asked.

"Yeah, I couldn't understand half of what you were saying!" Mike replied.

"Goddamn low battery." Dustin muttered.

"How many times do I have to tell you with the low battery?" Steve asked.

Tara winced; feeling a sudden sting in her arm.

She looked down at her arm and saw something moving inside of it!

"Well, everything worked out didn't it?" Dustin said sarcastically.

"Worked out? We almost died!" Erica exclaimed.

"That was only because Tara took an eternity to get help!" Steve replied.

"That's not her fault." Mike defended.

"Okay, Russians?" Lucas asked, bringing them back to the topic of russians. "As in, they're working for the Russian government?"

Tara clamped her hand over her mouth before she could let out a whimper. The pain was getting too much.

"What are you not comprehending?" Dustin asked with frustration. "Am I not speaking English?"

Tara glanced over at El and noticed her panting heavily.

"We have a full blown red dawn situation!" Dustin added.

Tara heard a very high pitch ringing in her ears. Her vision began to slowly blur.

Her hearing faded.

"So this has nothing to do with the Gate?" Max asked.

"This has everything to do with the gate!" Dustin snapped at her.

El dropped to the ground, collapsing right on the spot.

They all rushed over to her side.

"El!" Mike worriedly called as he rolled her over onto her back. "What's wrong?"

"My leg." El whispered.

Jonathan gently unwrapped her bandage and much like Tara's arm, there was also something inside of El's leg.

Tara tried to stay standing.

Her body went numb and she let out a low groan.

Her eyes rolled into the back of her head as she fell to the ground, passed out.

"'Tara!"

EIGHTEEN

Tara's eyes opened, and found herself laying in Max's lap.

Max's hand was stroking Tara's hair.

"Hey, shh, you're okay now," Max shushed Tara, her other hand caressing her cheek.

Tara blinked through her blurred vision, and found El screaming. El's hand was on Tara's arm and her own leg.

Two small creatures flew out of their arm and leg.

The creatures landed on the floor.

They began to slither away but a boot stepped on them.

Everyone lifted their heads up to find Joyce, Hopper and Murray.

They'd sat Tara and El up.

Tara's head was resting in Max's lap.

El's head was on Hopper's.

They were explaining to everyone what had happened.

"The Mind Flayer built this monster in Hawkins, to stop El and Tara and to kill her. And to pave a way into our world." Mike explained.

"And it almost did. That was just one tiny piece of it." Max added, her hand intertwining with Tara's.

"How big is this thing?" Hopper asked.

"It's big. Thirty feet at least." Jonathan replied.

"Yeah. It sorta destroyed your cabin." Lucas told Hopper. "Sorry."

Hopper frowned.

"Okay so just to be clear, this big fleshy spider thing that hurt the girls, it's some kind of gigantic weapon?" Steve asked which Nancy nodded to. "But instead of screws and metal, the Mind Flayer made its weapon with melted people?"

"Yes exactly." Nancy confirmed.

"I'm just making sure." Steve muttered.

"Are we sure this thing is still out there, still alive?" Joyce asked.

"El and Tara beat the shit out of it but yeah. It's still alive." Max replied.

"But if we close the gate again..." Will started off.

"We cut the brain off from the body." Max finished his sentence.

"And kill it. Theoretically." Lucas added.

"Yoo hoo!" Murray yelled as he approached the gang.

"Okay this is what Alexei called, The Hub." Murray explained. "Now, the hub takes us to the vault room."

"Okay, where's the gate?" Hopper asked.

"Right here. I don't know the scale on this but I think it's fairly close to the vault room. Maybe 50 feet or so." Murray said.

"More like 500." Erica said. "What? You're just gonna waltz in there like it's commie disneyland or something?"

"I'm sorry, who are you?" Murray asked.

"Erica Sinclair. Who are you?" Erica asked sassily.

"Murray Bauman." Murray replied.

"Listen Mr. Bunman; I'm not trying to tell you how to do things but I've been down in that shithole for 24 hours and with all due respect, you do what this man tells you, you're all gonna die." Erica said to everyone.

"I'm sorry, why is this four year old speaking to me?" Murray asked.

"I'm ten, you bald bastard!" Erica snapped back.

"Erica!" Lucas exclaimed.

"Just the facts!" She said.

"She's right. You're all gonna die, but you don't have to. Excuse me; may I?" Dustin asked Murray, gesturing to the piece of paper.

"Okay, see this room here? This is a storage facility. There's a hatch in here that feeds into their underground ventilation system." Dustin explained to everyone, while drawing his pencil down onto the paper. "That will lead you to the base of the weapon. It's a bit of a maze down there, but between me and Erica, we can show you the way."

"You can show us the way?" Hopper asked, with a hint of irony.

"Don't worry, you can do all the fighting and the dangerous hero shit, and we'll just be your navigators." Dustin compromised.

"No." Hopper said.

Will helped Tara up and they stood next to each other.

Joyce went up to them.

"Guys. I need to end this but I will be back before you know it, okay? You guys are gonna be safe there. It's far away from all of this." Joyce reassured the two. "Please stick close to Jonathan and do whatever he says."

"I'm not worried about me, Mom. I'm worried about you!" Will exclaimed.

"Oh honey, I'm gonna be fine." Joyce assured him.

Tara's bottom lip quivered. She could not loose any more people.

Joyce pulled the both of them in for a hug.

"I'm gonna be fine," She repeated over and over. "I'm gonna be fine."

Mike helped El walk after her goodbye with Hopper.

They hopped into the car.

A sudden car engine roaring gained their attention.

Billy.

Max's eyes went wide with the familiar feeling.

Tara squeezed Max's hand reassuringly.

"Back in the mall!" Nancy shouted as they rushed back into the mall.

"You're gonna kill him, aren't you?" Max asked sadly.

"I won't let them," Tara promised. "I'll protect Billy."

"This is just a precaution, okay?" Nancy said to Max.

"And not just against Billy. If he knows we're here then so does the Mind Flayer." Will told Max.

Nancy eyed the broken car that El threw.

"No chance that'll drive, right?" Nancy joked.

Tara raised an eyebrow with an idea.

Everyone began pushing the car. But even with all their strength, it wasn't enough.

"We can do it." El said.

"El-" Mike began with an exhausted sigh.

El threw her hand out, focusing on the car.

It wasn't working.

Tara threw her hand out as well, for extra help.

The car shifted a bit, but stayed still.

They groaned as it was too much for them.

They went with Mike's plan and managed to get the car down to its normal position.

"El." Tara spoke with a worried expression.

"I know. Come." El took her hand and limped over to a trash can.

El began to dig through the trash can until she pulled out one can of a Cola.

El placed it down on a surface and Tara nodded at her.

They both focused on the can, to crush it.

Tara found herself slipping into an old flashback as this happened.

Eleven and Twelve sat next to each other, their hands on the cold table in the Lab. Papa gave them a nod, signalling they could use their powers.

They started focusing on the can of Cola, and it wasn't long before the can crushed.

Twelve lifted a finger up to her nose and felt blood.

She looked up at Papa nervously, hoping she didn't fail another one of his tests.

He smiled at her.

"Tara? El?" Mike called.

The can had not crushed.

Tara's eyes widened at the realization. She had lost her powers.

Max raised her head upwards, hearing a faint sound she couldn't exactly pinpoint. She looked up at the ceiling of the mall. A loud THUD echoed.

"Mike!" Max called out.

Mike walked up to Max's side.

"Nancy!" He shouted.

Mike grabbed El and ran.

Max quickly grabbed Tara's hand and ran with her.

The Mind Flayer jumped down into the mall before letting out a loud screech.

Mike, El, Max and Tara huddled down behind a bar, hiding from The Mind Flayer.

"It's turned away. If we go up the stairs now, we'll make it." Mike whispered to Max.

"No way, not with El's leg." Max whispered back.

"There's another way to get out. Through the Gap." El whispered.

"Okay. Now." Mike whispered as he helped El up.

They bolted to the Gap, the first chance they got.

Tara stumbled over a vase and it smashed.

The Mind Flayer, of course, stomped over towards them.

Lucas shot at The Mind Flayer with his wrist rocket, giving the four enough time to make a run for it.

They made it outside, much to their relief.

But then they saw Billy.

Max quickly pressed a button, and the gate was closing. The gate to close off access to them and Billy anyway.

They started walking off into a room, with no idea that Billy was right behind them.

"Billy." Max whispered, loud enough to alert Mike, El and Tara.

Mike pushed El behind him.

Tara moved in front of Max, protectively.

Billy began walking towards Max, an aggressive look in his eyes.

Max quickly pushed Tara back, she knew what was going to happen.

"Billy, you don't have to do this. Your name's Billy Hargrove. You live on 4819 Cherry Lane." Max desperately told him, panicking. "Billy, please, I'm Max, I'm your--"

Billy swung his fist at Max's face, knocking her out cold.

Mike rammed himself at Billy, to protect El and Tara.

Billy threw Mike's head at the wall, knocking him out.

El threw her hand out but Billy easily grabbed El's head and knocked her out too.

Tara stayed still; frozen in fear.

He grabbed her head and slammed her into the wall.

Tara let out a weak cry as she passed out.

Billy bent down and picked up El and Tara. He slung them over his shoulder and began making his way back into Starcourt Mall.

Billy carried the two girls and laid them gently down on the floor.

El woke up first.

The first thing she saw was Billy whispering in her ear, "Don't be afraid. It'll be over soon. Just try and stay very still."

As her eyes adjusted, she noticed The Mind Flayer.

Her eyes enlarged as she panicked.

"Flay this, you ugly piece of shit!" Lucas said as he threw a firework at The Mind Flayer.

Everyone began chucking fireworks at The Mind Flayer, harming it, and delaying El and Tara's deaths.

But they soon ran out.

"Seven feet." El quickly told Billy, her eyes wide with fear. "You told her the wave was seven feet."

Billy froze.

"You ran to her on the beach. There were seagulls." El continued to tell him the memory. "She wore a hat with a blue ribbon."

Tara's eyes fluttered open. Her vision was still blurry. She couldn't make out what was happening.

"...A long dress with a blue and red flower. She was really pretty." El said as a tear rolled down her cheek.

"And you were happy," She said as she lifted her hand to stroke his cheek.

Billy's eyes fluttered close as he let her.

A tear rolled down Billy's cheek.

Billy stood up to face the Mind Flayer.

Tara's vision went almost back to normal but her head wound from where she was hit, prevented her from getting up. She felt pressure on her head.

Mike and Max ran out and saw all what was happening.

A tentacle came out of The Mind Flayer's mouth and headed straight for the two girls.

Tara closed her eyes, accepting her fate.

Much to everyone's surprise, Billy stood protectively in front of them and grabbed the tentacle.

"No!" He screamed as he pushed the tentacle back, saving El and Tara.

Max's eyes enlarged in shock.

A tentacle clutched onto Billy's stomach.

Billy let out a scream of agony. Of pain.

Several of the Mind Flayer's tentacles grabbed onto Billy, killing him.

Tara blinked her eyes in shock.

Blood poured out of Billy's mouth, he was in great pain.

A final tentacle attached itself onto Billy, therefore sealing his fate.

"Billy!" Max screamed in terror.

Billy fell to the ground, lifeless.

The Mind Flayer started screeching and thrashing around in pain, it was dying.

It soon fell to the ground, dead.

A fire started to erupt.

Mike ran to El's side and threw his arms around her.

El clung to him.

Tara forced herself to shut off her pain to go to Billy. She wasn't important right now.

She crawled over to Billy as Max slowly approached.

Max shook Billy's limp body.

"Please get up. Billy get up," She repeated as she shook his body.

"I'm sorry," Billy apologized before his eyes rolled into the back of his head.

He was gone. Dead.

"Billy," Max cried out.

"Max," Tara whispered softly as she pulled Max into her arms.

Max sobbed as she cried her heart out.

"It's okay, it's okay," Tara repeated as she tried to comfort the redhead.

NINETEEN

It had been a few months since the Battle of Starcourt Mall.

El had moved in with Joyce, and Tara couldn't be happier. After Hopper died, El needed someone familiar. She needed her sister.

Everyone was helping The Byers pack the house up.

"Turn around! Look at what you see!" Max, Tara and Lucas sang together much to Dustin's annoyance.

"Wait, did we get that verse right?" Max asked, teasing the Henderson boy.

"Yeah, but you're butchering it so could you please stop?" Dustin asked.

"So then join in, Dusty Bun!" Lucas said before blowing a kiss to him.

"Yeah, come on Dusty Bun! Why don't you join us?" Max asked.

"Dusty Bun, please." Tara begged with her puppy dog eyes she found Max couldn't say no to.

"You guys are so funny; you should be on Carson." Dustin said sarcastically.

"Can't we just hear your rendition?" Max asked. "Just one verse?"

"No!" Dustin said.

"Son of a bitch." Tara cursed. Son of a bitch was a phrase she learnt from Dustin.

"Y-You can't just use my own words against me!" Dustin said, his jaw dropped.

"Can." Tara said.

"Can't." Dustin said.

Lucas and Tara shot Max a look.

"Turn around. Look at what you see!" They sang again.

"Shut up you guys!" Dustin shouted.

"Max." Tara called as she stood up and extended a hand to the redhead.

Max took her hand with a soft smile.

Tara took Max to where her bedroom used to be.

"I wanted to say- I just-" Tara hesitated.

"What is it?" Max asked.

"Do you still love me? I have no powers now an-" Tara slowly spoke.

Max pressed her lips onto Tara's.

"You, Tara Byers, are the most important person to me. I love you for who you are." Max told her. "I will never stop loving you."

"I-" Tara began.

"I love you, okay?" Max said as she rubbed Tara's hand.

Tara gave a content nod.

"Oh hey, just to make sure you won't forget me," Max said jokingly as she pulled out a small box.

Tara gently opened up the box. Inside was a necklace with the initials of T and M.

Tara's eyes sparkled.

She gently took the necklace in her hand.

"I love it. Thank you." Tara said to Max.

"Want me to put it on you?" Max asked.

Tara nodded.

Max pushed Tara's hair off her neck.

Tara felt butterflies as Max's fingers ran over her neck.

Max placed the necklace onto Tara's neck and adjusted it perfectly.

Tara turned around and held Max's hands.

"I love you too." She said before her bottom lip quivered. "I don't want to leave you."

"We'll see each other again. And I promise, we'll have our sleepovers and movie nights and everything." Max promised her.

That made Tara content.

And it was time.

Time to go.

Tara hugged Mike, Lucas and Dustin and even Nancy.

She saved Max's hug for last.

"Goodbye Max." Tara whispered as she pulled Max in for a hug.

"See you soon." Max whispered back as they let go after a few moments.

Tara watched her friends' figures get smaller and smaller as they drove away.

Away from Hawkins.

Maybe this will be a good thing. A fresh start.

Time will only tell.

TWENTY

Tara felt a grin spread across her face as she heard the familiar sound of Argyle's vehicle.

Together, Jonathan, Will, Tara and El made their way outside, carrying school projects.

Tara, with a wide grin. She was beginning to love California.

"Alright," Argyle spoke. "Hold on to your butts, Brochachos!"

Joyce worriedly rushed out of the house.

"Slow down!" She yelled from concern.

Tara watched the pretty view of the mountains. She almost found it prettier than Hawkins! She liked to pick flowers. Her favorite flower though, was Rose.

They started making their way into their high school.

She smiled at El as the bell rang.

A redhead walked past and waved at them.

El waved back without realizing the girl wasn't waving at them.

Her smile dropped from embarrassment.

They made their way into their classroom, which was Show and Tell. About a historic hero.

They found their seats.

El jumped as a piece of gum flew at her cheek.

She wiped it off before rubbing it onto her desk.

Sure, Tara may have told Max in previous letters that she was fine in California, but truth be told, she was at her worst.

Her and El were being bullied, severely. It also didn't help that California didn't have any of her Hawkins friends. Or Max. She missed Max. Her freckles, her blue eyes and her voice.

"After learning to speak, she traveled the world to spread her message and along the way, changed how the world perceived those like her with disabilities. And that is why I have chosen Helen Keller as my hero." Angela said to the class.

The whole class clapped.

Tara enthusiastically clapped with a wide smile.

"That was wonderful, Angela. Truly wonderful!" Mrs. Gracey exclaimed as she turned to face her class of students. "What an inspiring story!"

"Okay. Now let's see who has to follow that." Mrs. Gracey said as she dug her hand through a jar of names on pieces of paper.

"Jane!"

The class slowly clapped.

El stood up to her feet and pulled up her project.

She walked towards the front of the class, putting on a brave face.

"Hi." El started off. "For my hero, I chose my dad."

Everybody just laughed at her.

"And for my visual aid, I made a direyama of our cabin." El said, while showing everyone her cabin structure.

"More like diarrhea." One boy joked.

Everybody laughed.

El faked a smile.

"Quiet, everyone." Mrs Gracey told them. "Let's be respectful."

El picked up the figure she made of Hopper.

"This is my dad. His name is Hopper, he made the best Eggos and we liked to watch Miami vice on Fridays." El said, recalling her favorite memories with him.

Then, El picked up a figure of a squirrel. Granted, one she killed.

"This is Mr. Fibbly. He is a squirrel." El told everyone.

Angela snorted.

Everyone chuckled along with her.

El inhaled deeply; trying to ignore them.

"And this is the alarm that my dad made. I-I was never scared because," El paused as she noticed Angela's hand up.

"Angela, let's save questions until the end of Jane's presentation." Mrs. Gracey told her.

"Yeah sorry, I'm just confused. I thought this was a presentation about a historical hero." Angela said.

"My dad was in the newspaper." El told her.

"Your local paper?" Angela asked with a chuckle. "I just don't think that's what Mrs. Gracey meant by historical. This is meant to be about famous people."

"My dad is famous. He saved lots of lives in a mall fire." El said, getting defensive. "He was a hero for people. And he was my hero too."

"That's not what I'm saying at all but it's okay." Angela replied innocently. "I am so sorry Mrs. Gracey. I didn't mean to interrupt. I just wanted to clarity on the rules of the assignment."

"Well, technically, you are correct." Mrs. Gracey confirmed. "But Jane has decided to do her father. So please continue with your presentation, Jane."

El fought back tears.

As soon as the bell rung, El was the first one out of the class, crying.

"El, it wasn't that bad." Will said, trying to comfort her.

"Friends don't lie." She told him.

"I'm not lying!" Will defended.

"El!" Tara called after her.

TWENTYONE

Argyle, Jonathan, Will, Tara and El sat at the airport waiting for Mike to arrive.

To say Tara, Will and El were excited was an underestatement.

Tara missed her friends so much, so even just seeing Mike, made her so unbelievably happy.

Her eyes laid on Mike, wearing a ridiculous outfit. He was dressed like he just went on a vacation to the bahamas!

El's eyes lit up and she waved at Mike.

"Mike!" She yelled with a wide smile.

She ran into his arms and he kissed her.

She hugged him happily.

"Oh careful; you're squishing your present." Mike told her as El pulled away from their hug.

Mike handed her a bouquet of flowers.

"It's a gift. I handpicked those for you in Hawkins." Mike said proudly. "I know you like yellow but now I'm realizing it's too much yellow. I know you also like purple so I got purple as well."

El's smile faltered as she read the name tag.

To El..

From Mike.

"They're perfect. Thank you." El thanked him.

Mike gave Will a quick hug.

"Hey, Tara." Mike said before giving her a quick hug.

"Hi." Tara said with a smile.

"That's a rad shirt, man." Argyle said, staring at Mike's shirt. "Ocean Pacific?"

"Oh hey Mike. This is my friend Argyle." Jonathan introduced.

"Oh Hey." Mike said before Argyle abruptly hugged him.

"Oh no," Argyle murmured as he let go of Mike. "No, it's a shitty knockoff. But don't sweat it. I'll get you the good threads out here."

"Hey, Mike?" Tara spoke.

Mike turned to her, relieved for that awkward conversation to end.

"How's everyone in Hawkins?" Tara asked.

"Uh, they're good. Lucas has joined a basketball team." Mike said. "We've made a new friend called Eddie. He's pretty cool."

"Oh." Will said.

"And Max? How is she?" Tara asked.

"Uh, I don't know." Mike shrugged. "Pretty annoying. She never shuts up about you."

"Uh, should we go?" Jonathan asked.

"Yeah, this is kinda awkward man." Argyle said.

"Yeah, so awkward." Mike said while moving to El's side and wrapping an arm around her.

"I have our whole day planned!" El excitedly rambled. "First, El rodeo for burritoes!"

"Really? Burritoes for breakfast?" Mike asked.

"Yes, trust me." El replied with a smile.

"No I trust you, it's just a little weird." He said.

"Then after burritoes, I want to go to Rink O Mania." El told him.

"What's Rink O Mania?" Mike asked.

"It's the most fun place in Lenora. They have skating and games." El replied.

"Sounds awesome. Are your friends going to meet us?" Mike asked.

"Friends? What friends?" Will asked.

El shoved Will.

"You know, Stacy and Angela!" El replied, while shooting him a look.

"Angela?" Will asked nervously.

"You'll meet them, I promise. Just not today. I want today to be about me and you." El said to Mike while leaning into him.

Mike gently kissed her forehead.

"Have fun." The woman said who gave them their rollerskating shoes.

"Thanks." Tara thanked her.

"Bitchin right?" El asked Mike.

"Yeah bitchin." He replied. "So do you come here a lot?"

"Yeah." El said.

"No." Will said.

"Yes and no." Tara replied, making their conversation more confusing.

"Will does not but Joyce makes Tara come to parties with me." El lied. "It's a big party place."

Will rolled his eyes.

They sat down to put on their rollerskating shoes.

"Oh, I forgot. You need socks." El told Mike.

"Oh." Mike said.

"They sell them at the counter." Will said.

Mike quickly rushed over to the counter.

"How'd you forget about the socks? I mean, since you come here all the time." Will asked El, sarcastically.

"I don't know. I just did." El replied.

Tara slid her feet into her roller skating shoes.

"Why do you keep lying?" Will asked.

"I'm not lying." El defended.

"You're not? You're friends with Stacy and Angela and you come to parties here?" Will said to El before turning to Tara. "And I've seen you writing your letters to Max, saying everything's fine. Do you really think she'd want a lie? Or would she want the truth?"

"I really don't think Mike's gonna like that you lied to him. When he finds out, he's gonna be mad." Will said.

"Okay so, I asked for vomit green and I got vomit green! How awesome is that?" Mike joked.

But nobody laughed at his joke.

"Mmmm," Mike licked his lips as he drank his milkshake.

"Milkshakes?"

A familiar voice exclaimed.

"Angela." Tara nervously spoke.

"Where oh where, have you been hiding this handsome thing?" Angela asked while fluttering her eyelashes at Mike suggestively.

"Angela, this is Mike. My boyfriend." El replied.

Angela extended her hand.

"Angela. Pleasure." She said as El looked down uncomfortably.

"I heard a lot about you. It's really cool to finally meet some of El- Jane's friends." Mike said after shaking her hand.

"Friends? Yeah! Super cool," Angela said before pulling El up to her feet. "Come on friend. Let's skate, shall we?"

Angela pulled El off to the roller skating rink.

Will stood up, worry consuming him.

Tara gulped.

Her and Will noticed a boy carrying a camera.

"Oh no." Will muttered. "El hasn't been telling you everything. Neither has Tara but Mike listen. She's been having problems here."

"Okay, what kind of problems?" Mike asked.

"Angela is mean to her. To me." Tara admitted.

"Alright! This next song is dedicated to Jane, the local snitch." A man said as he played a song.

A group of girls began to circle El, and stuck her hand out, like El and Tara would do when they had powers.

"Freak! Go home!"

Tara clenched her fists angrily. Nobody hurts her sister and gets away with it.

The music suddenly stopped.

Then, a boy threw a drink over El.

She tripped and fell down.

Angela skated over to El's side.

"No food or drinks on the rink!" She said with a smirk.

El's bottom lip quivered.

"Hi." Tara growled s she skated over.

Angela spun around.

Tara raised her fist and clocked Angela in the face.

Angela yelped as she stumbled, dazed.

"Angela!" El said as she slashed Angela's face with her rollerskate.

Angela let out a scream as she fell to the floor.

Blood quickly dripped from Angela's nose, it was bad.

The two of them turned around and everybody was staring at them.

It was to protect her sister but Tara felt disgusted with herself. She hurt someone.

Mike and Will rushed over.

"What did you do? What did you do?" Mike repeated in disbelief.

TWENTY TWO

Once they got home, they were instantly greeted by the warm smell of food.

They saw Murray cooking.

"Well well! Aren't you lot a sight for sore eyes?!" Murray yelled enthusiastically at them.

Jonathan waved with a stoned grin.

"You kids like Risotto?" Murray asked.

"There I was, headed down the I-5, going to see a client in Ventura. I'm looking for a motel to stay for the night, and suddenly bam! It hits me! Didn't the Byers move here?" Murray explained.

"It's a small world." Joyce chuckled.

"So I thought why don't I drop in and say hello to my old friends?" Murray continued to explain.

"It's so sweet of you." Joyce said with a smile.

"Even sweeter of you to let me stay." Murray replied.

"And he cooks!" Joyce said.

"And cleans. Regular little housewife." Murray added.

Tara slightly smiled.

"You should just stay," Joyce told him.

"I'd be tempted, Joyce, except we have that business trip." Murray reminded her.

"Right, that business trip." Joyce said.

"What business trip?" Will asked.

"Oh my gosh, I almost forgot to tell you guys. This thing came up at work and it turns out I have to go to a conference tomorrow in Alaska." Joyce said.

Tara dropped her fork in shock.

"Alaska?" Everyone exclaimed.

"That's where they're based, the Britannicas. Joan and Brian Britannica." Joyce added.

"So do Eskimos still live in igloos or are they fully blown living in the suburbs now?" Argyle asked.

"Who is this?" Murray asked.

"So Jonathan, this means that you're going to have to take charge while I'm gone." Joyce told him.

"Wait. What?" Jonathan asked, looking disoriented and dazed.

"Oh my god." Will face palmed himself.

"Your mom's going to Alaska." Argyle filled Jonathan in. "The Britannicas are there."

"Jonathan, what is wrong with you?" Joyce asked with confusion.

"I think I know what's wrong with him." Murray hinted.

"We just had a super stressful day." Jonathan said.

"This girl got shmacked in the head today at the roller rink." Argyle said.

Tara's eyes darted around the room as her heart pounded from anxiety.

No.

Joyce would be so mad if she knew.

"Shmacked?" Murray asked.

"Yeah, it was one of those vicious skate attacks." Argyle replied. "Anyway, she looked like she was going to be fine."

"She didn't look fine." Mike replied coldly.

El rose to her feet and stormed upstairs.

Tara picked at her fingernails to avoid eye contact with Mike.

"What is going on, you guys?" Joyce asked.

"Okay, I sense tension." Murray chuckled. "Is it the Risotto?"

Tara shook her head no.

"This Risotto is schmacking, dude." Argyle complimented the meal.

"Still have no idea who he is." Murray commented.

The next day, there was a knock at the door.

Tara skipped to the door and opened it.

"Excuse me. Are you Jane or Tara Byers?" A man in uniform asked.

Tara's breath got caught in her throat.

She struggled to get a word out.

El came down the stairs and froze.

The cop grabbed Tara's wrists and placed a handcuff tightly around her.

Same for El.

"You have the right to remain silent. Anything you say can and will be used against you in a court of law. You have the right to an attorney. If you cannot afford an attorney, one will be provided for you."

The cops walked Tara and El out and put them in the back of a police van.

Tara quickly wiped her tearing eyes.

She never knew this would've happened.

The police van suddenly halted to a stop.

A cop walked to the back of the van and unlocked it.

El rammed the door open and pulled Tara out with her.

Tara stumbled, dragging El with her to the ground.

Two men grab the two girls, by their arms.

"No!" Tara exclaimed as she struggled against them.

A man stepped out of a van.

Tara's eyes widened as she recognized him.

Owens.

"Hey, kiddos!" He said.

Owens took them into a diner and sat down with them.

"Sorry about all the theatrics." Owens apologized. "I didn't mean to scare you."

"It's fine." Tara said.

"You certainly talk a lot more than when we first met!" Owens joked with her.

He then cleared his throat.

"You both got yourselves into quite the predicament, didn't you?" He asked them.

"You know I relocated you guys to Lenora because I thought, Safe town, small dull, far from Hawkins. Nothing could happen here! And what was it, a roller skate or something?" Owens asked.

Tara bit her bottom lip, her gaze on her fingers which rested on her lap.

"Ready to order some food?" A waitress asked.

"I'll have some more coffee, and," He turned to the two girls. "Whatever you want, it's on me."

"Waffles please." El said.

"Just a sandwich." Tara replied.

"Never too late in the day for breakfast, that's what I say!" Owens chirped.

"Am I in trouble?" El asked.

"For that roller skate thing? No, we'll make that go away. Don't even worry about that." Owens replied.

"That's not why you're here?" El asked.

"To be honest, I wish it were." Owens replied. "Last night I saw something. Something I've been dreading for some time. I don't know how to say this other than just to say it."

Tara nodded, urging him to continue.

"Hawkins is in danger."

"You've fought this evil before and you've won. But this evil is like a virus. Each time it returns, it comes back stronger, smarter, deadlier."

"A war is coming to Hawkins."

"But my friends are in Hawkins. My girlfriend is in Hawkins." Tara desperately said.

"I know. I also know there are good people, brave friends, who have helped you fight your battle in the past. But they alone can't win this war. Not without you."

"I know it's not fair to ask more of you guys but without you, we can't win this war."

El leaned closer in her seat.

"We don't have our powers." She told him.

"What if I told you there was a way to bring them back?" He asked.

Tara's eyebrow raised in interest.

"I feared this moment would come, so I've been preparing. Developing the means to restore both your abilities. A program that has the potential to not just bring them back, but bring them back stronger than before."

"But there are others who don't believe in you. Who think you two are the cause. I believe they're wrong. I believe you're the cure."

"That's why, if we're really gonna do this, I'm going to ask that you leave with me now."

"I want to try something. If one of you were to leave with me, and one of you went back to Hawkins, to warn them. You both are connected, your powers were strong. If one gets their power back, I believe the other will too."

"Our friends in Hawkins, are they in danger?" El asked.

"I'm afraid, your friends in Hawkins are very much in the eye of the storm." Owens said.

"I'll go back. To Hawkins." Tara decided.

"They're not the only ones in danger. It's life as we know it. This is why I'm here." Owens continued. "Because you two are our only hopes."

They exited the restaurant.

A woman hopped inside a car.

"You should reach Hawkins by morning." Owens told Tara.

"Good luck." Tara said to El.

Tara inhaled deeply before getting into the passenger side of the car.

And they took off.

TWENTY THREE

T ara's eyes slowly opened as she woke up from her nap.

'Welcome to Hawkins'

She realized she didn't have the foggiest idea on where everyone would be. She'd start with Mike's house.

"Um, can you take me to 2530 Piney Wood Lane? East Point?" Tara asked. She had memorized Mike's home address.

The woman nodded as she drove to Mike's house.

She pulled up the car and waited for Tara to get out.

Tara stepped out of the car and it wasn't long before the woman drove off.

Tara took a deep breath as she knocked on the front door.

Karen answered the door.

"Well hello there!" Karen said with a smile. "Oh you just missed your friends!"

"Where are they?" Tara asked impatiently.

"They said they were heading to the grave." Karen replied. "East of Haw kins."

Tara took off running.

"Max!"

Tara heard Dustin or Lucas yell her name.

She raced over to where the voices were coming from, and found Max levitating in the air.

She rushed over, panting.

Max's eyes snapped open and she fell down.

Tara threw her arms out and caught Max in her arms.

Max was hyperventilating and her eyes widened as she looked up at Tara.

"Y-You.. But I'm still here..." Max panted.

Tara slowly set Max down.

"I'm here." Tara assured her as she took Max's hand in her own.

"How?" Max asked.

"I heard... about what's happening." Tara said. "A war is coming to Haw kins."

Max's breathing was still heavy and she clung to Tara's hand.

"I'm here and I'm real. I promise you." Tara repeated over and over. "I'm here."

Tara was asleep on the floor of Mike's basement. Her head was on Dustin's lap.

"Wake up!" Nancy said as she shook Dustin hard.

Tara's eyes slowly opened as she let out a yawn.

"Sorry Tara," Nancy's eyes softened before she glared at Dustin. "Aren't you supposed to be on Max watch?"

"Yep, yep." Dustin said, rubbing his eyes.

"Then where is she?" Nancy asked.

Tara rose to her feet very quickly.

"Max?" She called out.

Tara raced up the steps and into the Wheeler's house.

"Max?!" She called out, getting more scared.

Nancy and Dustin followed after Tara, and Tara rushed into the kitchen.

Her breath got caught in her throat when she saw Max sitting down at the table with Holly.

"Morning guys. Everything okay?" Karen asked Nancy.

Tara walked up to Max with a smile and took a seat next to her.

"You're okay?" Tara asked.

"Yep. I've got you back again." Max said with a grin.

"California sucks." Tara whined.

"It's not that bad." Max defended before she gasped. "Oh, I forgot to give you something."

Max pulled out a paper envelope.

"This is, um, for you." Max said as she handed Tara the evelope.

"Don't open it now." Max told Tara before she did anything else.

Tara nodded as she placed the envelope inside her hoodie pockets.

Nancy came over and sat down next to Max.

"Is this what you saw last night?" Nancy asked.

"I mean, it's supposed to be. I thought it'd be easier to draw it out than to explain it but," Max's voice trailed off as Dustin came over, a mouth full of food.

Nancy pulled over a picture Max drew of Chrissy and Fred's bodies.

"It was like they were on display." Max said. "And there was this red fog everywhere. It was like a dream. A nightmare."

"Do you think Vecna's just trying to scare you?" Nancy asked Max.

"With Billy? Yeah. But when I made it here, I dunno, something was different. He seemed surprised almost; like he didn't want me there." Max said.

"Maybe you infiltrated his mind." Dustin said. "He invaded your mind, right? Is it that big of a leap to suggest you somehow wound up in his? What if you somehow unlocked a backdoor to Vecna's world?"

"Vecna?" Tara asked.

"Yeah, that's what we're calling him." Nancy said.

"Maybe the answer we're looking for is somewhere in this incredibly vague drawing." Dustin said, glancing at Max's drawings. "God, we need Will."

"Yeah no shit. But I tried Joyce's number again this morning and it's the same busy signal." Max said.

"It's probably Argyle." Tara said. "He's schmacking."

"Schmacking?" Holly asked.

Nancy suddenly frowned.

"Is this a window?" She asked Max. "Stained glasses with Rose."

"Yeah, see? I'm not so terrible after all." Max said to Dustin sarcastically.

Dustin shot her a look back.

"Yeah well, it helps that I've seen it before." Nancy said.

Nancy began folding up pieces of the drawings and once she was finished, they made all together, a drawing.

"It's pieces of a house." Max realized.

"Not just any house. Victor's house." Nancy revealed.

Nancy rose to her feet.

"Where are you going?" Dustin asked, his mouth still full of food.

"Waking the others," Nancy replied.

Tara yawned.

"Sleepy head," Max mumbled.

They pulled up the car at the Creel house.

The house was really boarded up.

"That's not creepy." Steve mumbled sarcastically as he walked up to the board covering the front door.

He and Nancy began unnailing the board.

"What exactly are we supposed to be looking for in this shithole?" He asked Nancy.

"We're not sure. We just know this house is important to Vecna." Nancy replied.

"Because Max saw it in Vecna's red soup mind world?" Steve asked.

"Basically." Nancy replied.

"Great." Steve said sarcastically.

"Maybe it holds a clue to where Vecna is. Why he's back; why he killed the Creels. And how to stop him before he comes back for Max." Dustin said.

Tara tensed up. She hated the thought of someone after Max, especially someone they knew nothing about.

"We don't think he's in there, do we?" Lucas asked slowly.

"I guess we'll find out." Max responded.

They managed to break the board down and it fell with a THUD.

Max stared up at the door, studying it.

Steve rattled the door knob but it was locked.

Tara let out a long sigh.

Robin abruptly cleared her throat so everyone would look at her.

In her hands, was a brick.

"I found a key," She simply said as she tossed the brick through the door, causing glass to shatter.

Steve reached his hand inside the door for the lock.

He unlocked the door.

The door slowly opened.

Everyone began pulling out their flashlights.

"Where'd everyone get those?" Steve asked. "Tara's been here for just a day and she has one yet I don't?"

"Do you need to be told everything?" Dustin asked. "You're not a child!"

Steve frowned.

"Hey guys?" Max called.

Everyone went over to her.

"You all see that, right?" She asked, pointing her flashlight at a grandfather clock.

"Yeah." They all said.

"Is this what you saw in your visions?" Nancy asked Max.

Max nodded, her eyes trained on the clock.

"I mean, it's just a clock." Robin said.

"Why is this wizard so obsessed with clocks?" Steve muttered. "Maybe he's a clock maker or something?"

"I think you cracked the case, Steve." Dustin joked.

"All I know is, the answers are here. Somewhere." Nancy murmured.

"Okay, everyone stay in groups of two. Three, if you must." Nancy instructed. "Robin, upstairs."

Robin saluted before following her.

"Lucas," Max called as she held Tara's hand.

Lucas, Max and Tara walked through the Creel house.

"Lucas," Tara said.

He turned around to her.

"I've missed you. A lot. And Dustin." Tara said.

Lucas smiled.

"I missed you too." He said. "Wasn't really Hawkins without you."

"Mike told me, you basket ball?" Tara spoke.

"Yeah, I did." Lucas said.

The lamp's light started flickering wildly.

"I promise I'm going to stop asking this but you're seeing this right?" Max asked.

"Yeah."

The light suddenly went out completely.

Instead, a different lamp's light switched on by itself.

Different lights in the house switched on and off.

Everyone gathered around a room, where the ceiling light was flickering on.

"It's like the christmas lights." Nancy said, causing Tara to smile at the nostalgic memory.

"The christmas lights?" Robin asked.

"When Will was in the upside down, the lights came to life." Nancy replied.

"And Lucas hated me." Tara recalled causing Lucas to shift uncomfortably.

Max shot Lucas a glare.

"Vecna's here." Lucas said. "In this house. Just on the other side."

The ceiling light went out.

"I think he just left the room." Robin said.

"Did he hear us?" Max whispered.

"Can he see us?" Steve asked.

"Max, music. Please." Tara said worried.

They all made their way up into the attic.

All their flashlights turned on by itself.

All of a sudden, their flashlights smashed in front of their faces.

They yelped.

Something out of the ordinary was happening.

TWENTY FOUR

"Not to be a wimp but can I sit in the car? Cause this is gonna totally and royally suck." Robin whined.

"It'll be fine." Nancy assured her.

"I just can't stand to see those doe eyes of Eddie's break again." Robin said.

"At least he can drink himself into feeling better!" Steve exclaimed.

"That's what my mom does," Max muttered as she played with Tara's hair.

"Oh shit," Nancy cursed. She pulled up the car to where everybody was hanging out at. With cops.

Tara gulped nervously.

"I think I'll sit in the car." She mumbled.

"It'll be fine," Nancy said again.

They got out of the car and got close enough to listen to what the cop had to say.

"...Little after midnight, reporting a homicidal on the lake. Officer Callahan and myself arrived first on the scene. We made our way to the shore of Lover's lake, about ten yards from that house you see behind me."

"It was there that we found the victim, an 18 year old senior from Hawkins High, Patrick Mckiney."

Lucas frowned with sadness.

"We have a serial killer on the loose. We have also identified a person of interest. Eddie Munson."

"Dustin? Can you hear me? Wheeler?" A voice Tara didn't recognize came from the walkie.

Dustin turned on the walkie and spoke. "Eddie? Are you okay?"

"Nah, pretty goddamn far from okay." He replied.

"Where are you?" Dustin asked Eddie.

"Skull Rock; do you know it?" Eddie asked.

"Yeah, that's near Cornwallis and-" Dustin began.

"Garrett. Yeah I know it." Steve said.

"I swear to god, if they get us lost," Max said aloud as they walked to Skull Rock. "I mean, that's bound to happe-- Woah!"

Tara tripped over a branch but Max caught her.

"You're so clumsy," Max chuckled.

Tara smiled back.

They made it to Skull Rock.

A noise behind them made them jump.

Eddie jumped down to them.

"You, Dustin Henderson, are a total butthead." Eddie said.

Dustin grinned and hugged Eddie.

"We thought you were a goner!" Dustin exclaimed.

"When I got to the shore, I tried calling you guys but my walkie was busted." Eddie told them. "So I did the thing that I do now. I ran."

"Do you know what time this was? The attack?" Nancy asked.

"Yeah, I know exactly what time it was." Eddie said while throwing Nancy his watch.

"9:27." Nancy said.

"Same time our flashlights went kablooey." Robin said.

"Which means what, exactly?" Steve asked.

"That the surge of energy was Vecna attacking Patrick." Nancy said.

"Well, we're one step closer. We know how Vecna attacks." Robin said.

"And where he attacks from." Lucas added.

"So now we just need to sneak into his lair into the upside down and drive a stake through his heart." Max said.

"If he even has a heart." Robin joked.

"A stake? Is he a vampire?" Steve asked nervously.

"It was just a metaphor." Max said.

"A bullet should work." Eddie said.

"I say we chop his head off." Lucas said.

"I'd say all of the above but we can't do any of that until we get into the Upside Down." Nancy said.

"We need El and Tara to get their powers back." Max said as she glanced at Tara.

"Everything was way easier. We had these girls, they had superpowers." Steve told Eddie while gesturing to Tara. "Speaking of, meet Tara."

Tara waved with an innocent smile.

"Hey." Eddie said while shooting her a grin. But then he frowned at Dustin.

"Hey, Henderson's not cursed?" He asked Steve.

"Cursed? No. Mental? Absolutely." Steve replied.

"Boom!" Dustin yelled.

Tara shot him a look.

"Bada bada boom." Dustin said to Steve. "I was right. Skull Rock was north."

"You're wrong!" Steve exclaimed.

"Yes and no. This compass worked correctly when we left the Wheelers and when we got in the car at Kerley. But it started to slip the further east we went." Dustin said. "Now it's way off!"

"So, you're using faulty equipment. You're still wrong!" Steve argued.

"Remember when I messed up your compasses?" Tara spoke. "I'm not doing it."

"Not like she can." Max said.

"Exactly. Either there's some super big magnet around here or..." Dustin's voice trailed off.

"There's a gate." Lucas said.

"But we're nowhere near the Lab." Nancy said with confusion written on her face.

"But what if, somehow there's another Gate?" Dustin asked. "A gate that we don't know about. It'd have to be smaller. Way less powerful."

"Snack size gate." Robin spoke.

"How? Why?" Steve asked.

"No idea. All I know is that something is causing this disturbance, and the last time we've seen anything like it, it was a Gate." Dustin said. "And I hope it is because then we'd have a way to get to Vecna. And a shot at freeing Max from this curse."

Dustin began walking off.

"Where are you going? We can't just go out for a hike in the woods! Eddie's still a wanted man." Steve exclaimed.

"This little steel capsule might be the key to saving both Max and Eddie. What say you, Eddie the Banished?" Dustin asked Eddie.

"I say, you're asking me to follow you into Mordor, which is a really bad idea. But the shire is burning. So Mordor it is." Eddie said, standing up to his feet.

Dustin bounced up and down with joy.

They followed the compasses to Lover's Lake.

"There's a gate in lover's lake?" Max asked.

"Whenever the Demogorgon attacked, it always left an opening." Nancy said. "Maybe Vecna's the same way."

"Only one way to find out." Steve murmured.

Steve and Eddie helped Robin onto the boat.

Then, Eddie and Nancy hopped on.

Dustin tried to get on but Eddie stopped him.

"Hey, you trying to sink us?" Eddie asked. "This thing holds three people, tops."

"It's better this way. Stay here with Max. Keep an eye out for trouble." Nancy told Dustin.

"It's my goddamn theory!" Dustin exclaimed.

"You heard Nance." Robin said.

"Who put her in charge?" Dustin asked.

"I did." Robin said.

Steve hopped onto the boat at the last minute as they began to take off.

"You said three!" Dustin exclaimed.

"Ugh," Lucas grimaced. "When'd Steve get so hairy?"

"Right! I keep telling him he needs to tame that jungle but he claims the ladies dig it." Dustin agreed.

"Let me see." Max asked.

Max took the binoculars and looked at Steve for a good few minutes.

"You guys realize, if there's a gate down there, it's technically a water gate?" Dustin asked with a giggle.

Behind them, they heard police.

"Shit down!" Lucas grabbed Max and Tara, pulling them down with him and Dustin.

"Cops." Max muttered.

"Shit." Dustin cursed.

"We can't let them find Eddie." Lucas hissed.

"Stay with me." Max said before standing up to her feet.

"Hey officers!" She yelled. "Over here! I found the killer! This way!"

Max grabbed Tara's hand and they all ran.

The cops were fast though.

Dustin tripped and fell to his feet.

A cop grabbed his arm, knowing the others wouldn't just leave him.

TWENTY FIVE

"What exactly were you all doing at the lake?" Officer Powell asked.

They looked at each other for a story.

"We were just going for a walk." Max lied.

"A walk? At 9pm?" Powell asked in disbelief.

"A schmacking walk." Tara said innocently.

"To the lake!" Dustin added in an overly high pitch voice. "We were gonna take a little night swim."

"Dusty! Someone was just murdered there." Dustin's mom exclaimed.

"Yeah, we didn't realize that until we got there." Dustin quickly said.

"That's why we didn't swim." Lucas said.

"And Nancy; was she with you at this night swim?" Karen asked.

"No." Max replied.

"Yes." Dustin said.

"Maybe." Tara replied.

"We're not sure." Lucas said.

"She was there but then she left." Dustin quickly said. "It's all a little confusing."

"That's when you guys came." Lucas told the cops.

"Right and then they dared me to say what I said, about the killer." Max said.

Dustin and Lucas fake laughed.

"You're lucky you didn't get shot." Ted grumbled.

"Have you had any contact with Eddie?" Powell asked.

"That psycho freak killer?" Dustin asked. "God no."

"No, we haven't heard from him." Max lied.

Lucas and Tara shook their heads no.

"We barley know the guy." Dustin lied.

"Who?" Tara asked.

"Oh, that's a bunch of bull!" Erica hissed.

"Erica!" Mrs and Mr. Sinclair exclaimed.

"I mean, you realize their lying? The whole couch is on fire." Erica said.

"Are you lying to these policemen, Dusty?" Dustin's mom asked.

"No!" Dustin exclaimed in a high pitch voice.

"Lying to the cops is a crime, son." Lucas's dad reminded him.

"I'm not lying!" Lucas defended.

"The fire is consuming us." Erica said.

Dustin and Tara glared at her.

"Threaten them with a little jail time. Maybe that'll loosen their lips." Ted suggested.

"You wanna send our kids to jail?" Lucas's mom asked with disbelief.

"We need to take this seriously." Ted replied.

"He didn't mean it like that." Karen said.

Everyone was arguing all at once.

"Shut up!!!" Powell shouted at the top of his lungs.

"One at a time." Powell said as he pointed to Max. "You."

"Wait, why me? I'm not even in the Hellfire club!" Max exclaimed.

"Do I need to cuff you?" A cop asked.

Max went silent.

Max walked into a spare room with the cop.

"You don't think they went through..." Lucas's voice trailed off.

"Through Watergate?" Dustin asked. "Without us? Without a plan? Without weapons? They wouldn't be that stupid."

Tara shot him a look.

"They must just be laying low because the law got us." Dustin added.

"The law?" Erica asked with a snort.

"Erica. Please go away." Lucas scowled at her.

"Here's the deal. Either you tell me what's happening or I tell Dustin and Tara what I found under your bed." Erica threatened.

Lucas went pale.

"Please no." Lucas begged her.

"Spill your guts, cowpuncher." Erica said.

"The serial killer is a dark wizard from the Upside Down. And we've been looking for him but he's in the Upside Down, which we can't reach. At least we thought we couldn't until we found a Gate at lover's lake." Lucas explained. "That's the reason we were there but these stupid cops grabbed us. And if you tell anybody about this, that's including Mom and Dad and Tina- Especially Tina... I will smother you in your sleep. Do you copy?"

"The smothering in my sleep part. Not much else." Erica said. "Why would they open up a Gate at Lover's lake. The commies."

"The commies didn't." Lucas replied.

"Then who did?" Erica asked.

"Erica you raised an essential question." Dustin started off. "How did Watergate open up? Only two gates have opened up as far as we know. One by El and Tara and one by the commies."

Dustin's eyes widened as if he had just realized something.

"Holy shit." He cursed. "There's one thing we've never understood. Which is why Vecna's killing people. What's his motive? Killing teens? It always just seemed too random."

"On top of that, how does the Mind Flayer fit into all of this?"

"How did El and Tara open the mothergate?" Dustin whispered.

"With our powers." Tara replied.

"No, like, you guys contacted the Demogorgon." Lucas said.

"With psychic contact! Just like..." Dustin said.

"Vecna when he casts his spells!" Lucas exclaimed.

"So, what if, with each kill; he's not simply killing them. He's making a powerful psychic connection with his victims?" Dustin pondered aloud. "A connection powerful enough to rip a hole through time and space?"

"He's opening more gates." Lucas realized.

"Why would he be opening more gates?" Dustin asked.

"To take over the world." Lucas said.

"Who do we know that wants to take over the world?" Dustin asked.

"The Mind Flayer." Tara said.

"So if the Demogorgon was just his foot soldier, Vecna's his five star gene ral." Dustin explained. "With the power to open gates."

"Holy shit." Lucas cursed.

Lucas had to explain to Erica.

"I'm listening, but you said you followed Vecna through lights? I think he's here." Erica spoke.

The light was flashing in a certain way.

"Wait. That looks like-" Tara said.

"S." Dustin said.

"O." Tara said.

"S." Dustin said again. "Hey uh, remember when I said they wouldn't be stupid enough to go through Watergate? I overestimated them."

They snatched Holly's light box and then plugged it in.

The light box turned on.

"You guys seeing this?" Dustin yelled out.

The light box vibrated.

Dustin giggled with joy and hugged Erica and Tara.

"We're not moving it but we're going to unplug it!" Dustin yelled out as Lucas unplugged the light box.

The light box formed a word. 'Hi.'

"Hi!" Tara exclaimed with a smile.

'STUCK.'

"Okay, they're stuck in the Upside Down!" Lucas realized.

"Uh, you can't get through Watergate?" Dustin asked.

'GUARDED.'

"Watergate's guarded?" Dustin assumed.

"Are you okay?" Tara asked.

'FOR NOW.'

"We think we have a theory that can help you get out!" Dustin called out. "We think Watergate isn't the only gate! There's a gate at every murdersit e."

'?'

"Come on!" Dustin groaned with frustration. "How many times do I have to be right on the money before you guys can trust me?!"

Dustin gestured to Max to come over to them.

They had sneaked outside.

Tara let out a long huff as she closed her eyes. They had such a stressful week. Started with all the intense bullying, the roller skating rink, Max and Vecna-

Cutting her off from her thoughts, a loud BAM! echoed.

Tara opened her eyes and saw the cop car's wheels had somehow burst. It was almost as if it was magically done.

"What the hell?" Erica asked as they all hopped onto their bikes.

"Tara, your nose!" Max exclaimed.

Tara felt her nose, and felt blood. That familiar feeling of blood.

"You have your powers back?" Max asked with relief.

"I-I don't know," Tara replied with a confused grin.

CHAPTER TWENTY SIX

They biked over to Eddie's house.

They poked through the ceiling with a stick and to their surprise, they found Robin, Eddie, Nancy and Robin through the ceiling. A gate!

Dustin giggled with joy.

Tara waved.

"This is trippy," Robin commented.

They pulled out a mattress and laid it down on the floor.

Next, they brought out a long sheet.

They set it nicely so that the sheet could be used as rope.

Robin came back first.

Next Eddie did.

They were waiting for Steve, but then they heard something that absolutely terrified them.

"NANCY!!!"

"Vecna." Max said.

Tara decided to see if she really did have her powers back.

She closed her eyes and teleported to Steve and Nancy.

It was correct. She had her powers back!

"Thanks Owens." Tara mumbled to herself.

Tara ran her hand down Nancy's arm to her hand.

She held Nancy's arm gently but firmly.

She closed her eyes and went into Nancy's mind.

To her horror, Tara found herself in the Lab.

She froze, terror consuming her.

There was blood painted on the walls. Dead bodies.

She heard a scream that shot her out of her fear.

She raced down the familiar hallways of the Lab and into many different rooms.

She threw open a door, and found Nancy, restrained in a chair by vines. Vines tying her ankles and wrists down.

There was a tall monster towering over Nancy.

Vecna.

"I want you to tell Eleven and Twelve...." Vecna told Nancy as she whimpered in fear.

"Tell her yourself." Tara spoke from behind him.

Vecna slowly turned around.

She flung him to the wall with her mind.

He glared angrily at her. "It's you."

Tara tossed the vines off Nancy with her mind.

"So nice to see you again." He said sarcastically as he struggled against the wall.

"A-Again?" Tara stammered.

"You don't remember me?" Vecna asked. "I'm hurt."

"If you hurt my friends again, I will kill you." Tara promised him as she closed her eyes, bringing her and Nancy back.

Nancy gasped, falling backwards into Steve's arms.

He caught her with incredible reflexes.

Tara teleported back to Max and the others.

"You're back," Max said, referring to Tara's powers.

"We have to go back there into the Upside Down." Nancy said once she had calmed down.

"Nope!" Eddie immediately said.

"We barley made it out of there!" Steve exclaimed.

"That's because we weren't prepared! But this time, we will be. We'll get weapons and protection. We'll go through the gate, find his lair and kill him." Nancy said.

"Or he'll kill us." Steve said. "He's not scared of us!"

"And for good reason. We were wrong about Vecna. He's basically like a sick, evil, male, child murdering version of Tara and El with really bad skin. But my point is, he's super powerful. He could turn us inside out with a snap of his fingers. It's not a fair fight." Robin rambled.

"So why fight fair?" Dustin asked. "You're right. He's sort of like Eleven and Twelve, but that gives us an upper hand. We know their weaknesses. Tara, you know that when you remote travel, you go into a trance like state?"

"No." Tara said. "Didn't know."

"Well you do now!" Dustin said. "What if Vecna's the same way? When he attacks his next victim, I'll bet you he's back in that attic, physical body defenseless."

"Defenseless? What about the army of bats?" Steve asked.

"True, we'll have to find a way past them." Dustin said.

"That all sounds great but we don't know when he's going to attack next. We don't even know who!" Robin said.

"Yeah we do. I can still feel him. I'm still marked. Cursed." Max said. "I ditch Kate Bush and draw his focus back to me."

"Max." Tara said while grabbing her shoulders. "You can't."

"I survived before. I can survive again." Max said confidently.

"I'm coming with you. Okay?" Tara asked her. "I won't let him hurt you."

"I just need to keep him busy long enough so that you guys can get into that attic. Then, you can chop his head off or stab him in the heart. Or even blow him up with some explosive Dustin cooks up; I honestly don't care how you put this asshole in his grave." Max said. "Whatever you do, try not to miss."

"I think," Steve said while rubbing his neck nervously. "Tara would kill us if we missed."

"Yes." Tara said instantly.

They had a plan. This was the time of year when people went camping.

So, someone ought to have a camper van.

Tara held the owners in place, stopping them from moving, with her mind.

They pushed open a window and jumped inside.

Tara followed soon after and released her hold on the owners.

They had successfully broken into someone's property, someone's vehicle.

Steve drove with Nancy in the passenger seat.

Max, Lucas and Tara sat together, by the window.

Lucas cleared his throat to get their attention.

"So I've been thinking," Lucas started off. "Two of the three of Vecna's victims were seeing Mrs. Kelley right?"

"Yeah," Max responded.

"So I figured there's a good chance Vecna cursed another one of her students. We go back to her office, we read her files. Look for mention of headaches, nosebleeds, nightmares," Lucas said as Max sighed out.

"We identify his most likely next victim." He said.

"Lucas," Max said firmly.

"We stake out his house." He continued.

"Lucas stop." Max said. "We don't have time for any of that, okay? And even if we did, even if our plan did work, we'd be putting a total stranger at risk. A stranger who has no idea what they're up against. I do. Plus, Tara will be with me."

"What did Vecna do to you?" Tara asked softly.

"He uses my memories against me. But only my darkest memories. It's like he only sees the darkness in us." Max explained. "So, I'll just run in the opposite direction. Run to the light. And maybe he won't be able to find me there. He won't be able to find us."

Max gave Tara's hand a reassuring squeeze.

"Now, how exactly do you plan on doing this?" Lucas asked Max.

"I'm not sure," Max admitted. "But it's my mind. Not his, right? So I should be able to control where I am. I just need to push him away. Find a happy memory and hide there. Hide in the light."

"You got a memory in mind?" Lucas asked.

Max nodded with a smile.

"It was a time when I was the happiest," Max replied as she glanced at Tara. "I'm always happy with my girl."

Steve, Robin, Erica, Nancy and Max went out into a store for hunting things to get weapons, while Dustin, Eddie and Tara stayed in the caravan.

"Guys?" Tara spoke.

Dustin and Eddie turned their heads to her.

"I'm going to see El and fill her in on everything." Tara said. "Tell Max if I'm gone long."

Eddie slightly nodded in understanding.

Tara closed her eyes and thought of El.

She reopened her eyes and did not recognize her surroundings.

She was in some sort of... room? It had a large tank.

She turned around, and nothing could've prepared her for what she was about to see.

She saw El (with shaved hair, mind you) and an all too familiar figure from her traumatic past.

Papa.

He blinked his eyes in surprise at her as El continued to speak.

"...If you try to stop me, I will kill you-" El paused as she noticed Tara.

Tears fill Tara's eyes in shock and fear as she pressed her back against the wall.

Brenner had tears in his, although that was from El's previous speech.

"Twelve," Brenner started off.

"Tara," She corrected coldly.

"Move, please." El asked Tara.

Tara stepped aside and her eyes were trained on Brenner's. She was terrified and confused.

El threw her hand out and soon after, the door fell down.

Brenner snuck up behind the two girls and plunged a syringe into their necks.

El threw her hand out, tossing Brenner to the floor.

Tara reached up to her neck and pulled the syringe out.

Her vision was slowly beginning to blur.

She glanced at Brenner, who was dazed, laying on the floor.

She took this as an advantage. And so did El.

El lifted him in the air and pinned him against the tank with her mind.

Tara angrily tilted her head to the side, and Brenner's wrist began to snap.

He screamed out in agony and pain.

Tara's vision blurred more and she began to sway on her own feet.

Her eyelids fluttered, as she tried to snap Brenner's wrist completely.

She could hear it cracking.

Her eyes rolled into the back of her head as she finally lost consciousness.

She fell to the floor with a THUD.

TWENTY SEVEN

When Tara finally awoke, her head felt foggy. And she was disoriented.

She recognized the feeling of laying on a bed.

But something was different.

Brenner injected a syringe into her neck once more but this time, only injected a little. He didn't want her to pass out. He wanted her calm.

"It's only a precaution, Twelve." Brenner told her calmly. "Just relax..."

He turned to El. "I very much hope our fighting has come to an end."

He turned back to Tara.

Coming back to check on El was a bad idea. She realized that now.

Brenner strolled over to her side and gently stroked her cheek with his thumb.

"Shh..."

Tara whimpered again, feeling frozen in fear.

"Shh," He said. "You have to understand that it was the only way. The best way."

She was back to being his lab rat again.

A tear rolled down her cheek as she realized something else.

He had taken her hair.

The alarm suddenly went off and Brenner froze.

"Eleven, Twelve, we have to go," He said, tensed up.

"W-why?" Tara asked, sitting up in the bed.

Brenner lifted both of them up into his arms, carrying them bridal style.

"They've come to kill you." He explained.

Tara was indeed drugged up but that didn't prevent her from doing something. She closed her eyes, teleporting to Max and the others presumably.

She reopened her eyes and found herself at the Creel house.

Tara took a deep breath as she looked around.

Erica's eyes widened. She'd never seen Tara teleport before.

"Tara- Oh no." Lucas exclaimed as he glanced at her appearance.

Max frowned as she looked at her girlfriend.

She reached up at her hair. "You look-"

"Badass?" Tara asked quietly before falling forwards into Max's arms.

Max caught her in her arms, managing to break her fall.

"I got you," She repeated, as she helped Tara stand. "I got you,"

"What's wrong?" Lucas asked.

Tara just clung onto Max.

"Are you ready?" Lucas asked Max.

Max nodded as she walked with Tara by her side, Erica and Lucas following behind.

They walked around with lights in their hands, trying to find Vecna.

Tara felt less drugged up now, but Lucas was with her, to keep an eye on her.

They sat down on the couch, as Erica rushed off outside.

Max.

Max spun her head around, puzzled that she heard her name.

Max. Remember I told you I'm telepathic?

Max's eyes widened as she realized it was Tara.

Tara smiled back.

Everything will be okay. I promise. When I kill Vecna, we could sleepover?

Max nodded with a confused smile. This was all very new and weird to her.

Lucas watched them.

They saw a bright light outside. Erica's flashlight!

They rushed over to the window.

Lucas flashed his flashlight back at her.

Max shot Tara a look as she reached down to her Walkman.

She slowly turned her music off.

Tara felt a lump in her throat. She didn't want Max to do this. This was dangerous.

"Hey, asshole!" Max yelled out. "I'm here."

"No more music. No more games." She added.

"Do you hear me?"

"What are you waiting for?! Do you want me or not?!" Max yelled out.

The light faded before going out completely.

They saw a new light go on, and went up into the attic.

Max set down her light and took off her walkman and headphones.

She sat down, hugging her knees.

"I thought about what you said. How I wanted my brother to die," Max started off. "I thought you were just trying to upset me. To anger me."

"But you weren't, were you? You were just telling the truth."

"Billy, he made my life living hell. Every chance he got."

"So sometimes, when I would lie in bed at night I would pray that something would happen to him. Something awful."

"I knew that he drove too fast so I would imagine him crashing. Dying in that stupid car."

"I wanted him out of my life. Forever. I wanted him to disappear."

"The day that he died, I think that's why I just stood there and watched. Not because I was scared or weak, but because I didn't know if he deserved to be saved."

"And I've tried to forgive myself. But I can't."

"Now, when I lie in bed at night, I pray that something will happen to me. That something terrible will happen to me."

"So that's why I'm here. Because... I just want you to take me away. And I want you to make me disappear."

"Wow. Really?" Tara asked, frowning.

"Hey, Tara. Why are you talking?" Max asked softly.

"Do you want me to disappear?" Tara asked, glaring at the redhead.

Max quickly stood up. She never meant to hurt Tara.

"No. Never. I'd quite happily sacrifice my life for you. A million times," Max quickly rambled. "And I'd do it again over and over."

"Oh, we're lying now are we?" Tara asked through gritted teeth. "Where were you when Billy was about to end my life? Hmm?"

"Tara..." Max spoke as she took her hand.

"Did you want me to die? Our love was all a myth. It was like everything else in this world, all a lie. A terrible lie!" Tara snapped at her as Max released her hand.

"Tara, you don't mean that. I can explain, honest. I love you," Max said, her eyes watering.

"Remember how I said I'd be there to save you? No. I think I'll let you die. It's what you want." Tara said coldly. "It will all be over soon."

Max started backing away. Something about this felt... wrong.

"In fact, I'll help him. I'll do it myself!" Tara continued as she seethed in anger towards Max.

Tara's voice went distorted and her eyes went white with no emotion in them.

Max whimpered; this wasn't her Tara.

"Your time's up!" Tara exclaimed as she raised her hand.

"No!" Max yelled as she grabbed her light and smashed it into Tara's head.

The disguise faltered, revealing Vecna himself.

Max took advantage of her short window of time and bolted out of the attic.

Max bolted down the stairs and dashed over to the door.

It was boarded up!

"Where are you going, Maxine?~" Vecna called after her.

Max rushed off towards another room.

Every exit seemed to be boarded up.

She frantically pulled at the boards but her attempts were futile.

Max pulled another door, which was a memory.

The door turned out to be the sauna, with Billy inside.

"Max!" Billy yelled angrily. "Let me out of here!"

"Open this door!"

Max stared at the hallucination-Billy in shock.

She was trapped.

Vecna was approaching.

"Tara," Max whispered. "Where are you..."

Billy threw his fist through the door and glass shattered.

He rammed himself against the door, trying to force it open.

Max gulped, frightened.

Max closed her eyes, trying to find a memory to hide in.

Memories flashed in her head, ranging from California ones, her first day at Hawkins, and... the Snowball dance.

She thought back to her first kiss with Tara, their first dance.

She admitted she liked Tara.

She'd do anything to go back to that day.

Max opened her eyes and she was at the Snowball Dance.

She grinned.

"Holy shit," She commented in awe.

Their song was playing as Max sat at a table.

She checked her watch. She'd been there for a few minutes now.

A loud POP! behind her caused her to jump out of her seat.

Flowers and balloons popped everywhere.

The song suddenly changed, into a 1940's one.

The colors on the walls started to change.

It was no longer bright and colorful. But rather, dark.

The flowers withered.

Ash fell down from the ceiling as Max watched.

Thunder roared.

Max dragged chairs over to the door to protect herself.

She turned around to drag another chair, but as she turned to the door, the chairs were gone.

The door had turned into the one at the Creel house too.

Vecna had found her.

The door slowly creaked open.

Max froze in place.

"You can't hide from me, Max," Vecna told her.

Max closed her eyes again, finding another memory.

She decided on the memory when she took El and Tara shopping.

"You think I don't see what you're doing?" Vecna asked her.

"You think I don't see everything? You thought you could trick me? You thought your friends could stop me?"

"I see them. I see your friends."

"Just as clearly as I see you."

"I can feel them dying."

Max's eyes snapped open and she was still at the Snowball.

But Vecna was nowhere to be seen.

"It's time, Max." Vecna told her as a clock chimed.

Max glanced around and saw no sight of him.

"It's time," Vecna repeated as he was behind her.

She spun around, eyes enlarging with fear.

He put his hand out, throwing her at the wall.

Max cried out in pain as she hit the wall, stuck there.

Vecna approached her.

Max whimpered.

"You are brave, Maxine." Vecna spoke. "Much braver than your brother."

"But in the end, you are weak and fragile just like him. Like all the rest of them."

"And you will break."

Vecna lifted up his hand above Max's face.

But he got flung back, away from Max.

Max hit the floor hard.

She was dazed from the fall but lifted up her head.

To her surprise, she found Tara walking into the Snowball room, her eyes trained on Vecna.

She held her hand out, keeping him in the air.

Vecna growled at this.

"Twelve." He seethed at her.

Tara didn't respond but threw him at the wall.

But she didn't let him go.

She kept throwing him at walls before finally tossing him aside with her mind.

That would keep him dazed for a bit.

Tara ran up to Max's side and helped her up.

"Hello," Tara grinned.

Max's eyes widened.

"I-Is it really you? Tara?" Max stuttered. She didn't know if this was her Tara.

"It's me." Tara said as she held Max's hand in hers.

Max stroked Tara's cheek, she believed her.

She let out a long exhale of relief.

"You came for me," She whispered.

El also ran up to them.

"El, you're real?" Max asked.

"I'm real." El assured her.

"How're you-" Max asked, her head slightly spinning.

"I piggybacked from a pizza dough freezer." El replied casually.

"What?" Max asked, frowning with confusion.

They heard a sound behind them. Vecna was regaining his strength.

He was royally pissed off now.

"Stay back." El told Max.

Max opened her mouth to protest.

"Stay. Back. Please." Tara cut her off.

Tara and El began to slowly approach Vecna.

"You will not touch my girl." Tara spoke firmly.

"Or we will kill you again." El added.

"Is that what you did? Did you kill me?" Vecna asked, finding humor in their situation.

"I am so glad you are here, Eleven and Twelve. It's just like old times,"

"This is going to be beautiful." Vecna started to raise wood into the air with his mind. "And it's all thanks to you both."

A faint red hue came into Tara's eyes. She was not going to let Vecna touch Max.

Vecna threw the wood at them.

Tara threw it back at him, with her mind.

Vecna easily dodged them.

He threw his hand out, tossing Tara aside.

Tara landed at the wall, dazed.

Vecna moved on to El and dragged her around on the floor. He then threw her up onto a table.

He threw her down to the floor, next to Tara.

Tara raised her head up, regaining her strength.

She slowly got to her feet but Vecna tilted his head to the side, bringing her back down.

Max rammed herself at Vecna, a stick in her hand.

She yelled out, focused on protecting El and Tara.

Vecna easily threw Max. She hit the wall and went unconscious.

"No!" Tara exclaimed in anger and worry.

El had risen to her feet but Vecna held her in place, and choked her with his mind.

He did the same to Tara.

Tara sputtered and coughed, needing air.

"Before I kill the both of you, I want you to watch." Vecna spoke as he opened the gateway to his world.

He threw El and Tara into the gateway.

They landed on the wet ground.

Tara recognized the red fog from Max's drawing she did earlier in the week.

Vines found their way onto both girls, and brought them up onto a tree.

The vines restricted around their limbs, restraining them.

Then, she saw Vecna carrying Max's unconscious body over his shoulder.

He dropped her onto the ground.

The vines brought Max up to the tree and restrained her too.

"Papa is dead." El suddenly spoke.

Vecna froze. He wasn't expecting that.

"I know what he did to you. You were different. Like Tara and I," El told him with tears in her eyes.

Vecna approached her and Tara.

"And he hurt you. He made you into this. He is the monster, Henry. Not you." El told him.

"You're right," Vecna agreed. "You two and I, we are different. And Papa did hurt me."

"But he was no monster. He was just an ordinary mediocre man." Vecna said. "That is why he sought greatness in others. In you and me."

Vecna brought his hand across Tara's cheek, frightening her more.

"But in the end, he could not control us. He could not shape us. He could not change us."

"Do you not see, girls? He did not make me into this. You did."

"At first, I had believed you sent me to my death. To purgatory. But I was wrong. I was somewhere new. I became an explorer. An explorer of a realm unspoiled by mankind."

"I saw so many things. And one day, I found the most extraordinary thing of all. Something that would change everything."

"I saw a means to realize my potential. To transcend my human form. To become the predator I was always born to be."

"No..." Tara realized.

Vecna nodded.

"It was always you?" El stammered in shock.

"All I needed was someone to open the door. And you both did that for me. Without even realizing it."

Tara felt sick. Papa wasn't the monster. No, she was.

"And when you did realize, you chose to resist. So I sought a means to open my own doors. I sought your powers."

"Once again, you both have freed me."

"Please. You don't have to do this. Just... let Max go." Tara begged through tears.

"It is over, Twelve. Your friends have lost." He told her.

A tear rolled down Tara's cheek. She knew she lost.

Out of the corner of her eye, she saw Max gaining consciousness.

She began to thrash against the vine's hold.

"Hawkins will burn and fall. And the rest of this senseless, broken world. And I will be there to pick up the pieces when it does. And remake it into something beautiful."

"You may not remember this, but there was a time when I hoped to have the two of you by my side." Vecna said. "But now I just want you to watch."

Vecna walked back over to Max.

Tara watched with tears in her eyes.

Another vine wrapped around her throat, suffocating her.

She couldn't breathe.

But she could honestly care less about the pain.

Her focus was on Max.

"Don't be afraid." Vecna told Max. "Try and stay very still."

"No," Max whimpered.

"It will all be over soon," Vecna told her.

Vecna lifted his hand up to Max's face once more.

"MAX!" Tara screamed out.

It was like Tara was frozen. She couldn't move, she didn't want to.

She was in shock.

She felt the vine around her neck and her limbs begin to loosen, somehow.

Vecna fully placed his hand onto Max's face, beginning to take her.

In the real world, Max's left wrist snapped. Then her right ankle. Her other wrist snapped.

Blood poured out of her once blue eyes, and down her cheeks.

El let out a scream as she broke herself and Tara out of their vine restraints.

Tara snapped out of it and her eyes went completely red with anger.

She threw her hand out, throwing Vecna with all her strength.

He fell back against a tree, groaning out in pain.

She wanted him pain.

Her eyes held a murderous and dangerous look in them.

"You and your friends believe you have won. But this is only the beginning. The beginning of the end," He said through gritted teeth in pain. "You have already lost."

"No. You've lost." Tara growled.

Vecna suddenly cried out in pain.

Fog surrounded them.

Everything around them began to fade.

"No, no," Tara whispered before yelling. "I have to kill you!!"

Tara reopened her eyes, she was back in the attic at the Creel house.

Max fell into Tara's arms as she woke up from the trance.

"Tara," Max croaked out.

"Yes. I'm here. Please, Max. Don't leave me. You can't," Tara whimpered, cradling Max's body gently.

"I-I can't feel or see anything," Max spoke.

Tears ran down Tara's cheeks.

"Please stay with me. Please. Please." Tara repeated as she pressed a light kiss onto Max's head.

"Tara, I'm so scared!" Max spoke as she laid in Tara's arms.

"I don't wanna die! I'm not ready!" She cried out.

"I don't wanna go! I'm not ready,"

"No," Tara cried as she looked down at her girlfriend's body.

Max's eyes rolled into the back of her head.

"Max." Tara spoke. "Max!"

Max was gone.

Tara let out a scream of pure heartbreak.

"MAX!"

A sort of gateway began to open from the floor.

Lucas helped Max's lifeless body out of the way.

Jason wasn't so lucky.

Tara pressed her hand firmly onto Max's heart.

Come back to me.

She shut her eyes, using her powers.

Come back to me, Max..

TWENTY EIGHT

Tara sat by Max on her hospital bed.

It's funny.

Even unconscious, she was still beautiful.

"Max," Tara called softly. "Please come back to me."

"I read something somewhere. If you love something, set it free. If it comes back, it's yours. If not, it was never meant to be."

"We're meant to be." Tara whispered as she stroked Max's hand with her finger.

The door suddenly opened, and Mike, Will, El, Nancy and Jonathan walked in.

Tara sat up from the hospital bed and hugged them.

After their hug, El looked at Max's body.

"Do they know when she will wake?" El asked Lucas.

"No. They say she might not," Lucas replied as Tara fought back tears.

"Her heart stopped for over a minute. She died. But then she came back." Lucas said, frowning slightly. "The Doctor's don't know how. They say it's a miracle."

Tara smiled sadly down at Max. She was her miracle.

El sat down carefully next to Max.

"I'm here, Max." El spoke as she took Max's hand in hers.

"I'll be back." Tara whispered into Max's ear and she slowly rose from the hospital bed. "I promise..."

She nodded to El as they walked to the door.

They drove to El's old cabin.

Jonathan opened the door of the cabin and sighed. "Oh Jesus."

The place was trashed badly.

"Holy shit." Mike cursed in surprise. "This place is a total disaster!"

The roof had a gigantic hole, where the Mind Flayer had jumped through.

"Well, that's a bit of problem." Jonathan commented.

"I get we gotta hide the Supergirls, but this isn't exactly the Fortress of Solitude." Argyle said. "It's more like a Fortress of Grodiness."

"Come on guys. I've seen Mike's room look worse than this," Nancy insulted Mike's room.

"Oh, brutal dude." Argyle said.

Nancy turned on the water before turning it off again.

"Ah! See? Water still works." She said with a smile.

She pulled down a box.

"Cleaning supplies!" She said.

They had cleaned up the cabin to the best of their abilities.

"Did she talk to you at all?" Will asked Mike, referring to El.

"Not much," Mike replied. "I mean, a little."

"Dr. Brenner. He said that she wasn't ready." Mike said, causing Tara to tense up. "And now she's starting to think that that he was right."

"That's crap." Will commented.

"I know," Mike said. "She's just never lost before. Not like this."

Tara nodded in agreement.

"You guys'll have another chance." Will said to Tara. He knew what she was thinking.

"Let's hope not. Let's hope One is-" Mike started.

"Vecna." Tara corrected.

Mike sighed at her.

"Fine. Let's hope that Vecna is dead and rotting." Mike finished his sentence.

"He's not. Now that I'm here in Hawkins. I can feel him and he's hurt." Will said as he shuddered with teary eyes.

Tara felt an odd feeling in her suddenly rise. Like, something bad was right next to them. She couldn't exactly pinpoint what though.

"He's hurting, but he's still alive," Will said. "It's strange, knowing now who it was the whole time but I can still remember what he thinks; how he thinks. And he's not going to stop. Ever. Not until he's taken everything and everyone."

"He's taken enough from me," Tara mumbled quietly.

"We have to kill him." Will said.

"We will." Mike assured him.

"No, I will." Tara said, seething angrily. "Taking Max was the last straw. I-I have so much anger in me and,--"

A glass bottle suddenly smashed.

"Woah, Tar." Mike murmured softly as he placed his hand on her shoulder.

A familiar man entered the cabin.

Tara opened her mouth but Hopper pressed his finger onto his lips.

Tara got the hint but nodded in his direction.

Hopper went into El's room.

www.ingramcontent.com/pod-product-compliance
Lightning Source LLC
Chambersburg PA
CBHW070349200726
48294CB00003B/809